EMBERS AMONGST THE FALLEN

Speculations

Colleen Anderson

Published by Naiad Publications

ISBN: 978-0-9881545-4-4
ISBN-13: 978-0988154544

Cover Art: Eric Warren
Creative Touch Design Group
http://www.creativetouchmt.com

For Dennis, who seeded my mind when I was a young explorer, by leaving all those science fiction books, like breadcrumbs to follow.

CONTENTS

ACKNOWLEDGEMENTS

This book has been many years in the making and the people who helped critique along the way made my work better. I appreciated all those editors who saw fit to publish my stories over the years, from that first one in *Tesseracts 3*. Even a reprint collection needs some helping hands. Thanks to Sandra Kasturi of Chizine Publications for being generous enough to proofread this, and give her opinions from a publisher's perspective. Eric Warren offered his creative services in designing the cover and I love what he did. Wayne Sallee and Steve Vernon were kind enough to add their comments and they are both seasoned dark fiction writers. I recommend looking up their work. Last but not least I must give credit to Ray Bradbury and Edgar Allan Poe, who helped shaped my mind when it was malleable clay.

INTRODUCTION

We Canadians are a crazy kind of people.

It might be the climate. All of that cold and that white and the winter that comes down like a blanket of Stay-Froze-Popsicles.

It might be all of that space. I mean—we've got nearly ten million square kilometers of geography—divided amongst a population of about thirty-five million people. That gives each of us a theoretical elbow-room of about a third of a square kilometer.

That's a little like living in your backyard – instead of your living room. All of that clean air and pure water is just bound to go to a person's head after a while.

Maybe that's what happened to Colleen Anderson.

Left out too long on the glacier flats – the cold ate down into her brain and crystallized her thought patterns – each synaptic response as individual as the uncountable snowflakes.

You doubt my words?

Just take a look at that first story of hers in this collection.

That one that calls itself "An Ember Amongst the Fallen." I first came across this story in a Nancy Kilpatrick collection entitled *Evolve: Vampire Stories of the New Undead.* The collection, put out by Edge Science Fiction and Fantasy Publishing, was an all-Canadian take on what the vampire was evolving into. I was lucky enough to have one of my own stories included in the collection—but it wasn't half as well-crafted as Colleen's work.

Colleen's story starts out with a wine snob.

Now I have known wine snobs and they are a very peculiar sort of animal. They live for the freaky complex articulation of the indescribable. The sort of dude that will sip a half-a-swallow of plonk and pronounce it to be both "jasmine and cigar box in anti-texture; a soothing blend of mimosa and kumquat—and just a trace of Aero Bar".

Only this wine snob isn't any ordinary wine snob.

This wine snob is a vampire.

I know, I know—you are saying to yourself right now that you have read every vampire novel and story and poem under the sun—although what any self-respecting vampire would be doing under the sun is WAY beyond me.

But think again.

From an innocent dalliance with wine snobbery, Colleen Anderson then evolves her tale into a combination of animal husbandry, the life-and-death style of vampire hip-chic, a religious system that neatly flips the standard tropes of good and evil – along with a smattering of vampiric eating disorders ultimately leading to the transgressional guilt-ridden spectacle of true unbridled vampiric sin.

Do you understand?

Colleen Anderson's stories are intricate and thought-provoking. They are unique and carefully-crafted with random snowflake brilliance - and before you commence to moaning and groaning something along the lines of—"Oh God, don't tell me I have to actually THINK while I read"—let me assure you of one more thing.

Colleen Anderson's stories are FUN!

So why in the hell are you wasting this precious reading time on my paltry introduction? Just turn the page and climb into that story and find out for yourself just what I am so excited about.

Dig in. Chew it up.

By the time you get done reading this collection you will be as weird as any Canadian I've ever met.

Yours in storytelling,
—Steve Vernon

AN EMBER AMONGST THE FALLEN

Shadows fluttered from the corners as Buer bit in just above the fine lines of the wrist and sucked. Only five swallows. No overindulgence before the dinner party, but that was much later. The blond male, lightly haired and slim, twitched but held still, his blood warm and slightly tart. Buer avoided the bull's stare and looked around the pen at the other beasts. He liked to keep the cattle clean and ready to drink at any point.

Some liked the taste better when the cattle fought but Buer found it made the blood acrid, sour upon the tongue and sometimes it stung going down. He preferred them docile, easy to subdue. The Book of the Fallen expressly forbade cruelty to or treating cattle as more than the meat and blood for which they were bred. Unpredictable, they could turn suddenly. Yet, if it wasn't for their musky smell and the rhythmic thump of their speedy hearts, they could almost pass as vampirii. It was their gazes that bothered Buer most.

He shuddered and licked the wound to help it close, then dropped the arm, smelling the tang of their oniony sweat. He checked the other stock in the wood-planked enclosure, the skylight now closed. The cattle liked sunlight and earthen tones. It was the one area of his condo that was not sleek metallic with black and blue accents. A plump white female steeped with red wine; every half hour a cup of pinot dripped into her bowl. A slimmer male paced in front of his white wine bowl. Buer pulled the list from his pocket and checked the time. He'd have to order the rest of the stock while at work. One calf still needed for the scotch. A fresh brown female raised on grains and exotic spices for the dinner. Oh yes; he had better grab a few rabbits for Jeanine. She was still adhering to her distasteful fad.

As he rolled down the sleeves of his white shirt, he locked the pen behind him, then looked in the fridge. There was enough cattle feed for later. Some flowers, an extra bottle or two of wine and he'd be set for the party. He pulled on the encompassing coat, the leather gloves, his shades and the wide-brimmed fedora.

He hated the season. Even with the protective clothing, he often itched at high summer. But it couldn't be avoided if he wanted to keep his job. Squinting, he hurried into the late afternoon sun and off to the lab.

Ronobe and Sammael barely noticed when Jeanine arrived, their hands entwined like hibernating snakes. Mystery slithered and slid about them, but Sammael only looked up long enough to accept the bloodwine that Buer offered.

Jeanine kissed his cheek and handed him a bottle. "Hello, my dears. Here, pour me a pure glass."

Buer took the bottle as Jeanine turned to Ronobe and Sammael. "Honestly, you two act like you just met. What's with you?"

Buer shook his head as he went to the kitchen. The troughs held the white freckled cow and a pale bull slumped and tethered beside each other on a large Naugahyde pad. He found Arkon drinking white bloodwine from the wrist of the bull. Arkon raised a black, winged eyebrow at Buer and smiled. "Sorry, I just wanted to see what you had on tap."

"Riesling from the Alsace region." Buer held up a bottle of sauvignon blanc. "I could pour you a glass of pure that Jeanine brought, or you could wait twenty while it decants." He popped the cork on to the mottled gray marble counter and tilted his head at Arkon.

"No, go ahead and decant it. I'll take a glass from this one." Arkon reached for a goblet on the counter, and with an elegant, sharp nail, punctured a vein in the male's arm; bloodwine dripped into the glass. The pale-skinned bull rolled onto his side, snoring. Arkon licked closed the wound and watched Buer open the enclosure door, and hook up the IV to a mesmerized calf in the first cage inside. The calves never liked the alcohol but their smaller bodies distilled it faster.

Buer checked the main course and the desert. The cow—exuding enough pungent cardamom, cumin and anise that it wafted off her sweating body—was riding the plump male bull. An astoundingly beautiful cow with long coils of honey gold hair stood nearby sipping from her bowl of port and watching wide-eyed. Buer had picked her and the port up as a last minute item to complement dessert. The pen would be well stocked for the next month. He had always found rutting cattle disconcerting but it kept them content. The hominid similarity was evident. Sometimes the Fallen didn't seem much different from their distant cousins.

Arkon said over his shoulder, "Do you really think you have a chance with her?"

Buer started, then turned and shut the door.

He put a pale hand upon Arkon's shoulder and walked back with him into the living room done in black with brushed silver and blue trim. "I haven't been able to forget about her for ten years. I have to try one last time."

Arkon just shook his head. "Give it up, my man. There are plenty to choose from. Besides, we're not meant for lasting relationships."

Jeanine, short spiky hair, model poised in lavender, stood at the window staring into the night. She was as pale as the moon's face. Buer handed her a glass of pure wine as the buzzer sounded.

The last guest called out as she entered in a swirl of emerald silk. "I hope you weren't waiting on me." Where many of the Fallen were willowy, she was all curves. Petite, with long, straight auburn hair, she had caught Buer's eye and heart the first time he saw her. They'd spent fifty years together, thirty of them tempestuous, but in the end her restlessness and his timidity had pushed the wedge between them. Like many vampirii, they learned to live with past loves being underfoot. There were always exceptions though.

Buer smiled and drew Camiel to the kitchen. "Not at all, my dear. We're just settling in. I'll bring out the main course soon. White or red?"

"You should know." She smiled at him and he punctured the freckled cow's wrist holding a goblet under the drip. The bloodwine slowly flowed in as Buer asked, "How are you? I haven't seen you in quite a while."

Camiel had opened the door and peeked into the pen. "Oooh, that looks delicious." She turned back, smoothing the green dress that outlined her exquisite body. "I'm good. Busy. Been flying to Paris and London a lot."

Buer had to look away, feeling his desire tighten his scrotum. "That's good. You still like the job?"

She shrugged. "So far. I think I'm good for another twenty before I'll try a new career. Still, I like the benefits of free travel."

He handed her the glass. "Go ahead. I'm going to get dinner ready."

As Camiel walked into living room, Buer stepped back to the pen and found the cow sleeping. He unlocked the cage and picked her up. She stirred but didn't wake. Laying her in the center trough of the table, he took a moment to clip her black hair short so it wouldn't get into the food. As he walked into the dining room he called, "Dinner's on."

They took their spots around the table, each person sitting into the scooped out spot that allowed close proximity to the hominid. A shallow blue porcelain bowl, with knife, spoon and fork sat beside each plate. Jeanine, so pale her blue veins threaded beneath her skin like lace, hung back, a look of disgust crossing her face.

Arkon rolled his bright blue eyes. "Don't tell me you're still on with this nutty thing about not eating hominids."

"It's not a fad, Arkon," she snapped back. "Can you say there is any difference between one of these and us?"

Camiel said softly as she sniffed the cow's arm. "Hmmm, they smell tastier. And it's brown."

Janine sat near the cow's feet, pulling at her sleeve. "Buer's wine vessels are as white as you and me."

Even Ronobe pulled her gaze from Sammael's angular face and dark intense eyes. She turned, solemnly saying, "Well, let's see, my dear. They lead short lives if left to the pasture. They can tolerate daylight. They don't seem to be able to talk—"

"That's not necessarily true. Primate studies have shown that they can be taught rudimentary language, even make some sounds amongst themselves. All primates show an understanding of sign language, and hominids can be taught simple tasks." She sipped her wine.

Ronobe laughed. "Until they turn on you. They're unpredictable."

Jeanine's lips thinned as Buer handed the long curved knife to Arkon. "Would you do the honors?" To Jeanine, he said, "I don't know, even dogs growl at each other. That doesn't mean they're intelligent. Besides, it doesn't seem right."

Arkon stood and the scraping of the chair awakened the cow. She looked around and started to sit. Buer grasped her head between his hands, staring into her wide eyes. She subsided again, looking dazed. Buer laid her back in the trough and sat between Jeanine and Camiel. The cow stared at the ceiling, mouth slack and open like a roseate flower. "All right," he said.

Arkon deftly cut into the jugular. The cow twitched and blood pulsed out of her gaping throat while she thrashed weakly. She gurgled for a few moments as blood threaded into the trough. Arkon had already sliced from belly to ribcage as she shuddered her last. "Preferences? Camiel?"

"Oooh, how sweet, first choice. I'd like the heart please." She dipped her finger in the trough and licked some of the blood from her finger. "Delicious."

Arkon deftly skewered the heart and put it on her plate. She ladled some blood onto her meat. He continued to cut the delicacies for each person: tongue, liver and eyes for Ronobe and Sammael.

The fad of the century was to eat meat with the blood, for its nutritive properties, but the lovers immediately played a game of passing an eye back and forth from mouth to mouth, kissing until one of them bit down, filling their mouths with juices as they both laughed. They looked like children with the red smears over their mouths and chins, which they licked away.

Buer went back to the kitchen and returned with a calmed rabbit. As he handed it to Jeanine, he said to Ronobe and Sammael, "What's with you two? You're acting as giddy as kids."

Ronobe, her hair a froth of wheaten curls, smiled as she chewed a piece of tongue, wiping at the blood that dribbled from one corner of her mouth. She pointed the fork at Buer and said, "Can't tell. Well…maybe at dessert."

Arkon, sitting across from Jeanine, made a show of eating the brain, smacking his lips and slurping blood noisily, but he spit the meaty bits out, having never been one to follow the current fad of eating flesh. "Hmm, are you sure you wouldn't want a piece of this? Very tasty. Spicy, hint of sweet. That mangy animal can't possibly taste good." Jeanine had broken the neck of the rabbit and delicately scooped only the blood with a teaspoon.

"I made my choice, Arkon. I'm happy with it. I can't drink hominids anymore. It's like eating a crippled cousin."

Buer sighed and shook his head as he cut into the thigh. She'd always found causes but had stayed with this the longest. "Next thing you know you'll be dressing them up in cute little suits and taking them to market with you. It's unseemly." Buer sipped the thick, heady bloodwine. It was a good mix, the fine wine and the pedigree of the cow. The bull with the white bloodwine had come from the same ranch.

Jeanine shook her head, her hair making her look a bit like a sunburst. "Please, Buer, there are limits. Someday, they may evolve into intelligent creatures. They do like to cook their food and use tools, and have been trained to work the fields in the last century. The anthropologists think we may have a common link."

"Sure," white-haired Sammael added, playing with Ronobe's curls. "If you believe the *Book of the Fallen*, then God sent Lucifer and his kind here where these hominids already lived, made in his image. But if that's the case, does God also look like a snake, a cat, an elephant?"

Jeanine shook her head. "You have to separate myth from scientific fact. Studies in language and primate behavior show similarities between vampirii and other hominids. Besides, God is known as the Great Deceiver."

Camiel's feral smile showed the tips of her fangs as she chewed through another chunk of heart. Of all of them, she took the greatest delight in eating as much meat as blood. "Be careful, my dear. Next thing you know you'll want to fuck the beasts."

Ronobe choked on a mouthful of liver. Silence fell over the table and Buer gulped down the rest of his bloodwine. Even Arkon had stopped chatting, staring wide-eyed at Camiel.

Jeanine sat as still as an ice sculpture, her spoon in hand as her face suffused with a pink luster. Then she turned toward Camiel and growled. "You have always been a self-indulgent bitch, Camiel, but I never thought you'd stoop to such horrific thoughts. Are you really so base as to not be able to discern the difference between an animal that shows possible forms of communication and intelligence and having to smear it with insinuations of bestiality? You disgust me."

Buer stood suddenly. "Ladies, please. This is supposed to be a pleasant dinner among friends. Does anyone want more? If not, I'll clear this away and bring out the dessert. Ronobe? Sammael? No. Anyone else?"

Jeanine still glared at Camiel who smiled and ate the rest of her heart. Camiel wiped her lips, which remained a deep lustrous red that Buer desperately wanted to kiss, working his way to her ample cleavage with love bites. He could still taste her cool, porcelain flesh after all these years.

He cleared his throat and unlatched the center trough, pulling the leftover meat into the cold storage pantry. There was enough for tomorrow's lunch. He drained the blood into containers, which he stored in the fridge. Then he brought the plump dessert bull from the pen. Mesmerizing it, he laid it in another trough and brought it to the table. Camiel had cleared the plates and filled two decanters of bloodwine.

Buer went back and tapped the vein of the calf for the rest of the white wine, and then brought out the cow filled with port. She meekly followed him and he tethered her in the living room near the gas fireplace, her amber skin shining in the fake firelight. She sat on the cushion and he left one of the others to mesmerize her while he went back for port glasses. "Help yourselves," he called into the icy silence still pervading the room.

He sighed and took a shot of scotch off of the other calf in the pen. Closing his eyes, he let the fiery drink singe him. Camiel always caused cold wars. But it was that coolness that had drawn him. How he wanted her.

Back in the living room, Ronobe and Sammael clasped each other's hands, sitting tensely on the edge of the sapphire blue couch, too wound up to taste dessert.

Arkon bit into one of the fingers, while Camiel fed on the opposite arm. Jeanine just sat back nursing her pure wine. Buer tasted from the bull's ankle and then poured port from the cow for everyone. She lay on her side as if asleep. He had to remember to feed the cattle the iron-rich paste before he went to bed. But later.

"Okay," Buer said. "What is it?"

Sammael glanced at Ronobe and nodded. Ronobe bit her lip, uncharacteristically hesitant. "Well, we know you might find this a shock, but we've been talking about this for years now." She paused as everyone sat looking puzzled. "We've decided to have a baby."

"What!" Jeanine blurted, looking even paler. "But—"

"Yes." Lean Sammael smiled. "We'll die."

Camiel shook her head, her brow creasing. "But why? Don't you enjoy life?"

Sammael smoothed back his nearly white hair. His unwrinkled face was as ageless as always. "When you have lived as long as I have, it…pales after a while. I have wanted a child for the last century."

Ronobe smiled. "I wasn't ready then. But we've activated our cycles now. It's exciting. The future has suddenly taken on a more intense hue."

Arkon just shook his head. "But your child won't get a chance to—"

"To what?" Sammael asked. "Our child will get a chance to continue the line or live forever, whatever it chooses."

Ronobe replied, "You forget. We all forget. Our parents did the same and were around for as much as a century after our births. And the sex is somehow…stronger."

Buer shrugged, looking at Camiel. Would she ever want a child? Ronobe and Sammael each had to trigger their reproductive tracts, which would kick in the aging genes: nature's control over the vampirii. Only an idiot started the process without a willing mate. Buer swallowed his bloodport and poured another, thick and purple.

Camiel glanced over and licked the rim of her glass. "Well, I wasn't going to announce this now but I can't let you two have all the fun." She pulled out an intricately carved silver moon on a chain. "I'm engaged."

Buer didn't hear the rest. The walls and chairs sucked away the sound. Everyone in the room seemed to recede. Mouths moved, motions slowed. What now? Camiel had been his beacon. She must care deeply if she was willing to marry whoever it was. Few vampirii bothered anymore. He would have bothered. Should have.

Numb, Buer saw Jeanine to the door, followed shortly by Arkon. Buer grabbed Camiel's arm as she swirled toward the door. "Are you sure about this?" At her look he elaborated, "I mean, I was hoping perhaps we could try again."

Camiel's laugh was more a short bark. She ran her fingers over her jaw. "It was fun, Buer, but you're too tame. You always follow the rules." Then she was gone. Out of his life.

He downed a couple more glasses of port and then shooed Ronobe and Sammael out, saying he'd clean up, congratulating them one more time, trying to smile before he locked the door.

He turned back and surveyed the room. The limpid sun was rising, its weak light barely penetrating the darkened glass of the apartment. In the light of the flickering flames, Buer flopped onto the couch. The bull still slumbered on the desert table, and the cow was sprawled to the right of the fireplace. He drank the rest of his bloodport. What would he do now? Follow more rules?

Buer stumbled to and fro from the kitchen, clearing glasses and dishes. He entered the pen several times and poured several large shots of bloodscotch until the calf showed signs of convulsing if he drained any more. He put the bull back in the pen and left some food for the animals.

Stumbling back to the living room, he pulled the curtains closed, took off his shirt and lay on the couch, every once in a while lifting his head enough to swallow more bloodscotch. When the glass was empty he let it tumble to the wood floor as he rolled off the couch. He crawled over to the cow and bit into a limp wrist.

Buer's mind fogged. He flipped over and found his head on a thigh. Kneading it, he bit into soft inner flesh, his fingers working upward. A quiet gasp reached him. Encouraged him.

Sucking some heady port blood, he closed his eyes and lapped, moving up to the juncture. With a moan, small hands grasped at his hair.

Camiel, always so lovely, so cool. He'd show her he could break rules.

But now she was heated. Her legs spread. He slithered up, his pants being pushed off. Nuzzling her neck, he bit lightly and slid slowly into her. She responded, moaning, wrapping her hands in his hair, her legs about his back, pulling him further in.

Buer groaned. "Camiel." His hands cupped her breasts and he moved rhythmically. As the pleasure built, his head filled with pressure as if his whole being was need and heat. Unexpected, fire flared almost painfully. A thrill of fear that he would burst into flames pushed him over, coming as she convulsed and bucked around him.

Buer groaned and threw an arm over his eyes, snaking his dry tongue over gummy lips. He stumbled off to the bathroom, scratching at his balls. Just as he began to piss he stopped, looking down at his sticky pubic hairs. A spear of ice lanced through him. Shaking, he pissed, then turned and stumbled back to the living room.

Lying where he'd left her was the hominid cow, staring up at him. She raised her pelvis to him. Buer ran back to the bathroom, spewing gory chunks of meat and blood into the toilet. Even after his stomach was empty, he heaved and gagged.

Shuddering, he rinsed his mouth. Pink pearls of sweat beaded his brow, rare for any Fallen. Lead filled his stomach as he clutched the edge of the sink.

What had he done? No. Maybe he had dreamed it. A nightmare. But staring at his come-sticky genitals he knew the terrible truth. The one taboo. Never to have sex with an animal, especially a hominid; punishable by death. He climbed into the shower and scrubbed himself clean till his skin shone pink.

He dressed, then reluctantly went to the living room, untethered the cow and put her back in the pen with the others.

Dusk set sullen and cloudy. It was early but he had to get away. Hunger knotted his stomach; he ignored it and hurried from his apartment.

Buer walked the streets, pacing up one and down another, disregarding direction or emerging shoppers. He rubbed his chin and hands, muttering, sorting what had happened. His mind skittered away from the abhorrent until he convinced himself of the alcohol's influence, the shock of Camiel's engagement. He couldn't bear the thought of going back to his apartment and the thought of meeting friends later for drinks made him squirm. Would they be able to tell what he'd done? Would the hominid smell still be on him? He sniffed at his hands, imagining he could smell port and the musky odor of female primate.

Eventually he wandered into an unfamiliar bar at an hour frequented by perpetual drunks. He glanced around at the lowest blue-collar types one step above the gutter. He sat at the bar and asked for a Glenfiddich but had to downgrade when they had nothing of that caliber.

The bartender drained a shot from the wrist of a young bull and put it on the counter. For a moment Buer stared at the row of cows and bulls, labels around each neck indicating the type of drink. Then he closed his eyes and shot it back, asking for another.

A scruffy, black-bearded fellow sat beside him, sewer tang wafting off him. He eyed Buer who ignored him, sipping his second bloodscotch.

The guy's gravelly voice rolled over Buer. "Looks like someone died the big death."

Buer just drank.

The guy leaned over, giving a quick glance at the bartender. "Hey, you interested in some Flare? Good stuff. Big rush. High lasts six hours, makes the world look like daylight."

Buer glanced over at him, shaking his head. "What…what would you do if you'd committed the unthinkable?"

The man's pale skin was pocked and dimpled oddly when he laughed. "Like what?" At Buer's look, the guy stood and backed away. "If you're a meat mater—"

Buer swallowed. "No. No, no, not that. I mean…cheating on your partner. Drinking too much." He broke into a sweat again, wiping it quickly away.

The guy laughed nervously. "Man, besides that nothin' is unthinkable. All been done before."

Buer heard nothing else and eventually the guy wandered off. After a couple of more shots, he left, but somehow the bloodscotch had not blurred his mind. The clarity of thoughts jabbed him. His stomach clenched at the thought of eating and yet he had remembered the warmth of the cow as she had enveloped him. A heat Camiel had never had. A fire that burned and soothed him. But then he'd been drunk. A terrible mistake. A nightmare. He would make sure the cow was used up by the next time he saw his friends. No one would know.

By the time he returned to his condo, it was daylight again. The sky's bloody tinges lightened. Buer hesitated outside the pen door. He pressed the button to delay the skylight's opening so he wouldn't be burned, and grabbed vegetables and beef from the fridge. When he entered he heard whimpering and looked down. Cursing, he knelt by the calf he'd left hooked to the IV for too long. Her red hair twisted in wet tendrils and she shivered. Pulling the IV gently from her bruised arm, he picked her up and unlocked the gate to the larger hold.

Staring at the two females and two males, he calmed them as he set the calf in. They would nurse her back to health. Then he put their food and the iron mixture inside.

He looked back and met each gaze, releasing them. The port cow was last and Buer flinched from her gaze. When he released her, she started to come toward the bards, hand raised, Buer backpedaled. He slammed the door shut and hit the skylight button.

His eyes squeezed tight; his heart seemed to twist. She was meat. It was revolting to do such a thing to a creature. Buer lurched to the cupboard, pulling out a bottle of pure scotch and sloshing it into a glass. He took two large gulps that burned their way to his belly but he could not dull the edges. Everything remained crystal clear. Rubbing his face, he staggered to the bedroom and dropped onto the bed.

The alarm had been buzzing for long minutes before Buer awoke, realizing he might be late for work. He had time to gulp down two glasses of cold blood before he left.

He immersed himself in his job, staying late each evening for several nights in a row, reluctantly returning home to feed the cattle and sleep.

Three days passed and Buer found himself drawn to watching the hominids as they slept and ate. The one female and the two males rutted often. The other, with long curls of amber gold hair sat alone, but once was forced to mate with one of the males. She screamed and clawed until Buer intervened, mesmerizing them all before pulling her out.

She tilted her head, looking up at him, a tiny smile playing her lips. He stared into her eyes as they glazed over, then leaned down and kissed the unresisting lips. Once Buer had laid her in the trough on the table, he went back and poured a glass of pure wine. Then he opened a vein on the cow's wrist and dripped the blood into the wine, watching the drops swirl and spread.

Taking two swift gulps, Buer stood with the sharp curved blade and leaned over her throat. She was truly beautiful, for hominid or vampirii. The knife clattered to the table as he admired the gentle curves of her body, the full breasts. Before he knew it he had reached out to stroke a breast. Buer gasped, pulling back, watching the rise and fall of the cow's chest.

This was taboo! There were rules, laws. The *Book of the Fallen* was explicit. Do not raise up the lesser creatures. Yet, the heat had been wonderful, soothing. Buer hadn't even realized he was stroking the warm flesh again. It was more than the yearning for the beautiful vessel. It was more. Far more.

He took her off the table and laid her on the floor as she slowly emerged from the mesmerism. "Aurora. Like the dawn." And Buer was as naked as the cow when he crawled over her, letting his cool flesh heat against her skin, his erection growing.

As he entered her, he felt the steady fast beat of her heart, his thrusts matching it. The cow gasped, moving beneath him.

Conflagration, of all-consuming heat that threatens to boil brain and eyes, evaporate flesh to papery ash. The contrast of fire with the moistness that whetted him brought Buer over the edge, gasping as his heart thumped two bass beats.

He pulled away from the cow's grasping fingers. The realization that his resolve had melted away sent him hurtling away to be lost in the warren of streets and bars. Eventually he had to return and found he'd left the cow loose.

"Aurora." He stood in the doorway watching her glistening flesh as she ran her hands over his art works, paintings, the couch, feeling textures. She turned and smiled shyly, then moved toward him. He held her at arms' length, looking through her, knowing now that when the Fallen had left God's light for darkness that the fall had not been complete. Buer was still falling.

She had lit a fire within him and this path lead to dissolution. Buer knew now what the Fallen feared, what the *Book* forbade. He took Aurora again, right there on the couch. She gave willingly and as he violently rammed into her, he tore her neck, drinking deep.

Her hands fought weakly against him and her death throes made him come hard.

He cried then. But survival mattered. Fires had been lit that could not be quenched. He stared at the gore of the ravaged cow as he changed clothes. He had broken the unbreakable rule, changed the stakes.

Buer unlatched the pen door, gathered his coat and left, walking into the dawn.

CONSUMING FEAR

Jenny has a black hole in her stomach. At least, she knows that's what it's called now. It is something dark that swallows all the bad things she's tasted. But like a black hole it also swallows the good foods she's eaten. She has had the black hole for a while now but Ms. Norton, in science class, just told them about black holes.

Ms. Norton said that even the men—and hopefully some women, Jenny thinks, who spend their lives studying black holes don't know exactly what they are. Jenny knows now that they swallow everything that's within a certain distance and that they exist in space. But, Jenny knows, it's a black hole that's inside her. In the space where her stomach is. Momma's always saying that she doesn't know where all the food goes that Jenny eats and Jenny isn't fat at all.

She frowns and pulls up on her shoulder bag full of books, and notices that she's only a house away from old Mrs. Kreiger's. Amongst the innocently yellow tulips the roses bite with thorns for purchase. Ivy wraps around strangely stunted and pruned cedar bushes. Jenny spots Mrs. Kreiger walking around the side of the house, hose in hand, watering her prizes. Scowling, Jenny loops her hands through the shoulder straps of her pack and runs past, not listening to Mrs. Kreiger's calls of, "Hello, Jen."

Instead, Jenny hums to herself and feels the bounce of her hair on her neck.

Home in a matter of minutes, Jenny bursts into the kitchen. "Hi, Momma!"

"Well, hi there." Momma smiles at her. "Dinner's almost ready. You want to go and wash your hands and set the table for me, please?" Momma's chopping vegetables for a salad.

The warm aroma of something yummy cooking, and the satisfying click click of the knife makes Jenny feel content enough to forget what's in her stomach for a few minutes. "Where's Dean? How come he isn't helping?"

Momma turns and smiles at Jenny, shaking her head. "You two, I swear. He's taking out the garbage and will clear the table after dinner. All right?"

Jenny nods, then runs up the stairs. She dumps her books on her bed then lathers rose-scented soap up to her elbows. Back downstairs she pulls sky blue plates from the cupboard and talks to Momma. "We had art and math and science today. Math was okay, but science was really cool." She puts three plates on the table knowing that Daddy's still out of town. Jenny runs her fingers around the rim of one plate and wonders if her black hole is large and shiny.

"Jen, I asked you what you did?"

"Jenny," she corrects. "Ms. Norton told us about black holes." Dean bangs in the back door but Jenny ignores her older brother and continues. "She said that they swallow everything in sight and nothing can escape them once they get too close."

Dean grabs a celery stick, deftly dodging Momma's swat, and lounges in one of the chairs as Jenny puts glasses and apple juice on the table. "That's what I have, you know."

"What?" Momma asks.

"A black hole. That's why I eat so much."

Dean snorts. "Geez, what a turnip head. Black holes only exist in space and it would have swallowed you up by now."

Jenny glares at Dean and states, "Well my teacher said no one knows everything about them and I have one in me. I know it!"

Momma sets the salad on the table and looks over at them. "That's enough, you two. Jenny just has a vivid imagination; it will help her remember the details. Now, let's eat."

Jenny sits and stares at her plate. Momma dishes up a helping of potatoes, beef and Brussels sprouts. She eats, thinking of her black hole, trying to enjoy the food while she can. The black hole will get it all too soon.

Dean grumbles but Jenny barely hears him. "Aw, Mom, I hate Brussels sprouts. Do I have to eat them?"

"Your sister's eating them."

"Yeah, but she eats everything."

After dinner, Jenny runs upstairs and leaves the dishwashing to Dean. She'll do them tomorrow. She lies on her bed and works out her homework on the solar system and the universe.

Dean stops on the way to his room and leans on the doorframe scowling. "Well, miss goody two-shoes-eats-everything. What a traitor. You used to hate Brussels sprouts as much as I did. Thanks a lot." He saunters off before she can say anything.

Jenny puts her book down and stares at the wall. Did they have Brussels sprouts for dinner? She knows she ate but as always, Jenny can never remember what she's eaten. Nothing. Not breakfast, not lunch, not dinner.... No smell, no taste, nothing.

She doesn't understand why the black hole doesn't swallow her up, but she's more convinced that it sits gnawing, persisting hungrily, like a baby sparrow waiting for food. If it was just Jenny eating she'd remember what food tastes like, what she's eaten. But she doesn't remember and she always feels light, almost buoyant. The black hole gets fed and is happy, not yet swallowing Jenny, just swallowing her memory of anything that enters her mouth.

She used to remember eating, when she was six. Even, she thinks, when she was seven. That was probably when she hated Brussels sprouts too. But something changed. Something dark and shadowy that made the black hole grow.

Sometimes—Jenny shudders and looks at the book's pictures of Jupiter and Saturn. Sometimes the black hole burps or something. Late at night, when she sleeps, she almost remembers what she has eaten. The tastes and textures come back, and the fear. A fear that chokes her throat and slides warm and heavily like slime into her belly. The bad things that enter her mouth. She awakes shivering and shaking but never remembers what scared her. She's kind of happy to have the black hole. If it wasn't for the black hole Jenny thinks she would be afraid more than just in her dreams. It does kind of make her special, too.

After homework and watching some TV Jenny burrows deep under her fuzzy blanket and dreams of puppies and windmills. The black hole keeps the bad tastes away.

Jenny's up, dressed in a blue dress with sailing ships on it and ready for breakfast while Dean still stumbles about in his room. Yawning, she says, "Morning, Momma."

"Morning," Momma smiles.

Jenny pours puffed wheat cereal into a bowl and milk on top. She spoons up mouthfuls and watches Momma sip coffee while wrapping blueberry muffins up in foil. Momma's dressed in a dark green skirt and jacket, ready for work and looks cool, for an adult. She puts a brown bag beside Jenny, and the muffins.

"Here's your lunch, Jen, and..."

"Jenny."

Momma sighs. "Jenny. And here's some muffins I'd like you to drop off to Mrs. Kreiger's after school."

Jenny feels the black hole in her. It seems to spin, rubbing against her insides, making her queasy. "Why can't Dean do it?"

"Because he has a baseball game after school."

"I don't like Mrs. Kreiger. I don't want to go." The black hole has already eaten all her breakfast. She can only remember she had cereal from seeing the box on the table.

Momma kneels down and looks into Jenny's eyes. "I know poor Mrs. Kreiger may be boring and old to you, but with Mr. Kreiger dying a year ago she's had very few people to talk to. She gets very lonely and a few muffins and a smile won't hurt you." She stands and pats Jenny's shoulder and is already walking toward the door with her briefcase.

Jenny's sniffing, trying not to cry. Why can't the black hole swallow her tears? But she knows it's because they don't enter her mouth. "She makes me eat yucky things."

"Like what, Jen?" her mother asks distractedly while fishing in her purse for her keys and balancing a mug of coffee and the briefcase.

"Jenny!" she almost screams. "It's Jenny."

"All right. Calm down. You're in a bad mood this morning." Momma stares at Jenny, one hand on the door. "What food is it you don't like?"

Jenny shrinks in on herself, shoulders hunching. "I don't know," she whispers. "I don't know." The black hole has chewed up her memory.

Momma looks at her watch and is already half out the door. "I have to go, dear. Look, if you don't like it just tell Mrs. Kreiger, no thank you. You don't have to stay long but be polite and give her the muffins."

Did Momma even hear her, she wonders?

Jenny trudges to school, knowing Momma does this whenever Daddy's out of town, Dean's playing a game, or Momma has to work late. Momma may want to be nice to Mrs. Kreiger but she also uses her to look after Jenny when no one's at home. Jenny hates it and would rather spend the time over at Kris's house playing with her dolls.

Jenny's day passes and she forgets about the muffins until she's putting her books back into her purple pack and encounters the crinkly foil. She thinks, *I could throw them away but Momma would find out and be so disappointed.*

Resignedly, feeling the black hole spin hungrily inside her Jenny walks up to Mrs. Kreiger's house. She's sitting on her porch reading a book as Jenny approaches. Her dress is a worn brown and she doesn't look lonely or poorly to Jenny at all. Her hair is thick and wavy, and silver, and her square chin is still strong if wrinkly.

She spots Jenny and puts down the book. "Well, well, Jen. Nice to see you. Come on up, I won't bite." She smiles from bright white and crooked teeth.

Jenny stands at the bottom of the steps looking up from under lidded eyes. "My mother sent something for you."

Mrs. Krieger's standing and stretching. Jenny lowers her eyes and rummages in her pack, pulling out the muffins and holding them out to her. She stares at the tulips.

Mrs. Krieger grins again and says, "Well, don't just stand there. Bring 'em in and we'll have some juice." She turns and enters the cool darkness of the house leaving Jenny no choice but to follow.

Jenny thumps her pack up the steps behind her. She stands just inside the door, smelling roses and mustiness. Mrs. Kreiger walks into the living room with a jug of lemonade and two glasses. She glances at Jenny but goes back to her kitchen for a plate of the muffins, their fat purplish berries looking like bruises.

Mrs. Kreiger comes back and pulls Jenny into the house, shutting the door behind her. "Come on in to the living room, Jen Jen, and tell me what you've been up to."

The living room is filled with shadows that seem to creep across the floor. Jenny swallows, dry-mouthed and sits on the edge of the old, worn burgundy sofa, as far from the old woman as she can. It rubs coarsely against her bare legs. Mrs. Kreiger pours her a glass of lemonade and all she can think of is pee. Mrs. Krieger passes her the muffins and she takes part of one hoping she will move away. Jenny bites into the muffin to avoid looking at Mrs. Kreiger and recognizes Momma's cooking. She tries to hold onto that thought, that comforting familiarity. She takes a sip of lemonade and it is only lemonade.

Mrs. Kreiger is asking about her family and she answers but wonders, *Why am I afraid? The food is okay. I wish I could remember.* The black hole seems to be bouncing around, banging her stomach so it flutters, and at her heart so that it beats hard.

"Well, Jen, would you like to see my parrot? Perhaps we can get her to whistle a tune."

Mrs. Krieger looks at her expectantly and she nods shyly. Mrs. Kreiger leads the way into the adjoining room. A big overstuffed chair rests near the cage that is on a high stand. The wires of brass curve gracefully together. The blue and green parrot cocks its head and whistles saying, "Hello, hello."

Jenny smiles.

"Here," Mrs. Kreiger's hands grab her about the waist and stand her on the chair. "This way you can see eye to eye with Flora."

Jenny thinks Flora is the most beautiful bird she's ever seen and watches its movements. Mrs. Kreiger talks about Flora and where she was born in the jungles. She talks about what they eat and how old the birds become.

Jenny is so rapt, looking at the bird, and what Mrs. Kreiger is saying, that she doesn't notice the wrinkled hand rubbing her bare legs at first. She tries to move away but the springy cushion of the chair makes her wobble. Mrs. Kreiger steadies her with the other hand and both touch her in ways she doesn't like. She can feel the black hole beginning to spin faster and faster in her stomach. It tries to swallow the fear that seems to bubble from her heart, her heart that beats like too many drums, but the fear is too large. It is making her shake.

Jenny pushes at the hands and says, "Don't. I don't like that."

"Shh, my Jen." Mrs. Kreiger smoothes her hair and presses Jenny into her body, nearly suffocating her. "You are so pretty, so young. It doesn't hurt to touch you. It doesn't hurt to hold you."

Mrs. Kreiger's working at her own skirt pulling it up and rubbing between her legs. "I won't hurt you. I have a lollipop...a candy for you. You'd like to lick my candy, wouldn't you, Jen."

"No," she shakes her head. "No, I don't want to. I— I have a black hole." And she can feel it pushing inside her, hungry for more, pushing in her throat, making her feel like throwing up.

She's somehow off the chair and standing on the floor but her head is at Mrs. Kreiger's waist. Mrs. Krieger's sitting on the edge of the chair and she's holding Jenny's head. "It won't hurt you. Just lick at my candy." She pushes Jenny's head toward her spread legs. Jenny struggles, her lips pressed firmly together. The food that tastes bad. The bad food. She's trying to force it on Jenny and Jenny doesn't want it, is scared. The black hole will take away the memory but Jenny doesn't want to touch her candy. She whimpers.

"Come on, Jen Jen," she breathes. "It's nice. It will feel good and make me happy. You want to make me happy, don't you?"

No, she doesn't and the black hole reaches up through the tunnel of her stomach and throat causing her to gag and gasp. Mrs. Kreiger tries to pull Jenny closer and Jenny feels the pull of the black hole. Jenny opens her mouth to scream but the black hole is there.

It sucks and swallows Mrs. Kreiger's legs and the skirt puckers as it goes into her mouth. Jenny watches, helpless, frozen. It's as if Mrs. Kreiger is a plastic bag with all the air being squeezed out. She starts to crinkle and shrivel as her eyes grow wide. She tries to pry herself from Jenny's mouth as the black hole swallows her chest, her arms. She compresses, falling in on herself. A thin wail comes out of the cartoonish face just before the black hole consumes it.

Jenny shakes, gasping in air. She gags and throws up but only liquid and half-chewed blueberries splatter the carpet. Flora shrieks from the cage, flapping wings, and seeds and feathers shower to the floor. No Mrs. Kreiger. Jenny looks about, dismayed. The bad food. Mrs. Kreiger was the bad food and the black hole has taken care of her. Jenny knows that she will not have to visit her any longer and goes to gather her pack.

She looks back at Flora and opens the cage and the window. Flora would starve otherwise and Jenny doesn't want that to happen. She quickly leaves, shutting the door behind her and runs all the way home, reciting the times tables in her head.

She can't think to do her homework and goes to bed without eating, feeling a queasiness in the black hole. The next morning Jenny barely touches breakfast before she goes to school. But school is the same. She feels heavy, bloated and senses the black hole churning now. Jenny remembers the half piece of toast she nibbled at breakfast and knows now what Mrs. Kreiger had done to her on each trip to her shadowy house. She now knows all that's gone into her mouth; the tastes, the textures. Jenny runs from the class and vomits.

She goes home early, ignoring the birds and flowers. By dinner she is hungry, a rumbling that challenges the black hole's churning. Silently she sits to eat the shepherd's pie that Momma has cooked. Momma watches quietly but Jenny doesn't look at her. The meal sits in her stomach like clammy lumps and seems to roll about. Jenny rushes to the bathroom and throws up. Momma follows her in as she gags over the toilet. "You poor thing. I'll put you to bed and we'll get you some broth."

"I don't feel t—too good."

Momma runs her hand over Jenny's brow, frowning. "You don't seem to have a fever but I think you better go straight to bed."

Jenny doesn't object and let's Momma wrap her in a flannel nightie too warm for the summer night. Momma sits holding her hand until she drifts away into sleep.

Jenny floats above a large black hole, suns and stars twinkling about her. The black hole is darker than the surrounding night and bulges as if something is trying to get out, and she hears Mrs. Kreiger's voice. "My Jen Jen, you take good care of me. You licked more of me than ever before. I'm in you now."

Jenny awakes shaking and whimpering, and tries to avoid sleep. But waking is not much better. The black hole is expanding. It makes her arms tingle and her head throb. Mrs. Kreiger was too much for it. The poisons in the woman are infecting the black hole and it grows and throbs like a large boil.

The next day and the day after Jenny tries to eat. Broths, soft eggs, juices, but nothing stays down. The black hole has taken all the room in her stomach, and constantly pushes on her throat causing everything to spew from her. Even the good tastes won't stay.

Momma sits on her bed on the third day and looks worried. "Jenny, I have to take you to the doctor. You're not getting any better. I should have listened when you said Mrs. Kreiger fed you bad food. I've tried to reach her but she doesn't answer the phone or her door. Do you recall what she gave you last, if you ate anything when over at her place?"

Jenny clears her throat and says, "I told you, Momma. There's a black hole inside me and it swallowed Mrs. Kreiger."

Momma doesn't say anything but leaves her room. She can hear Momma talking quietly on the phone.

Jenny goes for tests and more tests and this doctor and that doctor talk to her. They poke and prod and take blood. They never get near the black hole that makes it hard for Jenny to think these days. Finally, someone asks about the black hole and Mrs. Kreiger and she tries to tell them everything that she remembers. It is all she remembers now and her brain feels bruised and swollen.

Several days pass, unnoticed to Jenny. She has trouble forming words. Even her tongue feels thick, infected with the black hole. The blackness seeps into everything and muffles her. At last it is covering her, keeping her away from the memories. The hurt and fear are moving away, distant.

Back in the doctor's office Jenny is vaguely aware of words reaching her through the thick congealed coldness of the black hole. Like jelly. She wishes distractedly that they could remove it and Mrs. Kreiger from within her.

"Mrs. Cardston, most of the tests show that Jenny is suffering from malnourishment."

"You say most of the tests. What do the others show?"

"She's suffering from anorexia and what is looking to be a form of psychosis that will need further testing and therapy. As you now know, this Mrs. Kreiger, whom the police are still searching for, seems to have sexually abused her."

Jenny hears Momma's cries and her choked, "What does this mean?" Jenny doesn't respond. She is muffled, cold.

"It's affecting her mind and only time and therapy will be able to help her."

Jenny doesn't feel the arms wrap around her. She doesn't feel or think of Mrs. Kreiger. Jenny has a black hole in her head.

AMUSE-BOUCHE

n. Fr. (it) entertains (the) mouth

Elena leaned forward, on the edge of her seat, smiling at me. "I've waited a long time, my *petit chou*."

I said nothing, no longer interested in that flash of laughter in her eyes or those deceiving dimples on her cheeks. I closed my eyes for a moment's rest.

"Uh uh." She smacked the whip in her hand. "I want you to be part of this. No wandering off."

We both knew it a hollow threat. It wasn't the whip she would use.

Elena leaned close, staring into my eyes. "I hope you don't mind if I savor our time." She licked my ear, her tongue pointedly exploring each groove and whorl.

All I could do was moan as my mind slid to that moment I'd met her at the house party. She had impishly raised her eyebrow after Ben introduced us and said, "Ooh, I'd just love to eat you up. You're so cute." I'd laughed, embarrassed and intrigued.

A flush crept up her cheeks. "I hope this isn't too much for you." She kissed my lips, nibbling the edge and closing her eyes for a moment.

I swallowed, taking deep breaths through my nose. My thoughts traveled back to our day in the park. Elena had woven her way through the stark branches that clawed at the stormy sky as if tearing it with skeletal fingers. Then she'd disappeared when I had looked away.

I called, looking through arm-thick trees, then scurrying, calling again, confused. "Elena!" I shook my head and walked toward the darker copse of trees and brush. At the edge I peered in, shivering at the darkness. I looked behind once more, and there she was, petite, muffled in scarf and hat, staring at me. "Where'd you go?"

She had continued staring at me for a few minutes until I had finally penetrated her private world. Now I tried to find mine as I returned to the present. Elena ran her tongue between my fingers, sucking on the ends. I hadn't noticed.

She smiled softly. "I really do appreciate you."

I shivered and groaned, pulling at the ropes, but she had tied me well.

"Sweety, play fair. You men always come first. Now it's my turn."

Her damned sparkling eyes on me, she licked her way up my cock. I felt nothing but the gorge rise and I swallowed several times. Her full, burgundy lips kissed its length, then closed around the tip as it slid into her mouth. She bit, grinding her perfect teeth together as she severed the head. Chewing it down, she wriggled side to side, her other hand between her legs.

I glared hate. She reached toward the bowl. Instead, she stood and sauntered up to me. "Don't worry, babe. I save the best till last." She tapped my head. Then she went back to the bowl and picked up my lips.

She gave me that look again, as she had in the woods, no longer smiling.

WHAT STRANGE FRUIT

In shadows, I watched her for the third night in a row; unique even in this city of every scent and fashion. I strolled past crowded stalls strumming my lute, singing even here of the famous Coeur de Lyon, or I juggled, easily embedded in the frenzy and wild abandon of Constantinople. And always, I watched her.

I had not been here in centuries. The city had declined ever since that fool saw fit to rename it, and even now I saw that the Byzantine Empire would never equal the glory it once had. But Constantinople was still the heart we all flowed through, a glorious revelry of filth and splendor, chaos and order. It intoxicated just to stand in the middle of this vortex and watch the colors, smell and taste the aromas from every corner of the world.

I had come expressly for something new, different, and because I missed the sheer enormity of the place. Dancers and jongleurs, acrobats and whores, spice merchants and salt sellers; all manner of folk whirled about me. The life! If I stood still and listened long enough, I almost heard that ancient god of pandemonium's pipes playing from the hills as he inserted his will wherever he pleased, so much so that I wanted to take the whole city. So I pleased.

And this creature I watched, she had made Constantinople her home. If there were any original inhabitants they had melded into every other culture that summoned up the spirit of the city. Like sorry dogs sniffing a bitch in heat, my own kind also infiltrated. And I, I was both the mongrel and the bitch, circling those that challenged, and sniffing after them as well. That which slinked along the dark lanes and paths often picked off the scabrous morsels of humanity.

Richard's pummeling at Acre, and the battles before, had left enough detritus behind in the once great Byzantium to speed it on its decay. I gave it another century, no more. By then I would be gone, having plucked it of its last fruits.

I shook my head to clear it of cobwebby reminiscences, spun away from the stall I leaned against, and broke into song. "Peace delights me not! War be thou my lot! Law—I do not know save a right good blow!"

She looked up from the palm she held but her gaze lowered as quickly. I smiled and slid into an alley that torchlight didn't touch, to watch and listen. She was dark like the Saracen, but not one of them. Their women mostly remained indoors. It was hard to tell how much was the dirt and mud of road and how much her skin. Her clothes were a wash of colors enough to be the envy of any old emperor and disguise their dirtiness. In the oily guttering torchlight her full gathered skirt seemed a chameleon, first blood red, then deep blue, then royal purple. Beneath long unkempt and curling tresses I caught the glint of silver rings in her ears. Small bits of mirror or gems glittered like blinking eyes from her neck and skirt.

It was not the dress alone that drew me, nor her looks, though she had eyes as tawny as a mountain lion's. It's true I like to collect the unusual, and my home in Aragon held many rare treasures, never duplicated, and many never forgotten because none had seen them. This one was a treasure.

She was not alone. There were many like her about Constantinople, as dirty and chaotically patched together. There was something of their spirit I sensed, something uncageable, something strong. Not for centuries had I found creatures as intriguing or seemingly as powerful as these people who bore no special privilege. They displayed no richness, no superiority, no greatness of note, yet they held much.

Not many successfully train the great ursines to do as these people bid. I watched a shaggy lumbering beast rear up on its hind feet, towering several feet above the tallest man, and walk, or dance as they called it, in a circle. Where they had found the bear I knew not, but the man worked with it, not against it.

It is hard to get words out of many animals but my curiosity won through my caution. *Ho, ursine brother, what manner of beings are these that you walk with? What do they call themselves?*

His great unmuzzled head swiveled my way and he turned, dancing in my direction. I commanded him to stay where he was and answer. He did not say in words but his message was something like, *World-straddlers, like you, unlike you. Many names.*

I strummed discordance upon my lute and asked, *One name, give me one name.*

Rom—secret. Ascingani. He lowered to all fours and growled at the bedraggled bearded man who coaxed him.

The woman, barely so, sweet as ripened grapes, looked up quickly, her eyes meeting mine even where I shrouded myself in shadows. *She knows I spoke with her shaggy friend there.* World-straddlers—they touched both worlds and yet were mortal. I could not leave now, even if Saladin and Richard's righteous hordes came screaming through the gates.

I looked at the woman and her troupe again. I had to have one.

Like a cat teases the mouse, pouncing and tossing it before the eventual consuming, I like to play. Sometimes I play too much.

The next night I walked in illusion. The night was young; a faint pink still touched the western sky as the stars sprung out in the east. I tottered along, my shoulders stooped and head low, yet I beheld everything while looking at nothing. I noted him before he became aware of me and I moved away cursing. He was big, barrel-chested; a long mustache covered his mouth and obscured the roundness of his face. The almost jovial aspect did not lessen the dead black gaze of his eyes. He cared not that his stance, arms crossed, unmoving in the middle of those who came and went, caused many to stop and gape. He stood well over six feet and wore the bulky fur-trimmed clothing of the Huns and Magyars. Red and black brocade, heavy felted wool, and thick sheepskin boots. Even in cool winter air his clothes would be too warm for many.

I have less love for others of my kind than I have for most humans. They are tedious, wearisome, and think that domination is all that matters. The hunt, the game, the savoring of all aspects of life, yes, to the last morsel, that is what is enjoyable. The cold Magyar types are too brutal and lack finesse. I've crossed their paths in the past and they've crossed me. Yet, I do so love a game that gains layers and intricacies as it progresses. He watched my prize. I would show myself to him soon enough, but not yet.

I wandered past the fishmongers. The fetid musk of decaying flesh cloyed the air as it intermingled with spilled wine and sharp cheese. I breathed in, relishing the underlying tangy scent of stirring blood. Flesh is wonderful too; tasted, licked, sniffed. I like to savor my meals.

The woman wore her usual chameleon colors. She was reading a noblewoman's palm, holding it in one hand and running her fingers over the lines. But she looked into the woman's eyes and gauged much there.

Eventually, for I had all night, I approached the Ascingani fortune teller from behind and waited quietly. When she finished, the noblewoman looked momentarily surprised, then a tight smiled pressed her lips and she dropped copper coins into the reader's hand. As the Ascingani woman turned she almost stepped on me, and stopped. Her hand flicked up to her heart, her breath momentarily catching.

In all the nights of watching I had never seen that look. She recovered quickly and asked, "What do you wish, old woman?"

"My fortune. I seek my fortune, sweet…girl," I wheezed. "What lies in store for an old widow like me? Will I see my sons again?"

She sniffed and pushed her hair behind one cinnamon brown ear. Her eyes momentarily unfocused, then she focused on me again, frowning. "It takes silver to see the future."

"Silver I have," I replied and held one coin between my fingers.

Money is the one true ruler and she nodded her head once, then held out her hand. I dropped the coin in it and she reached for my hand before I knew it. But just before she grabbed it she pulled back. "Come." She pointed to some muddy black tents. I hesitated. She replied softly, "I have a crystal that can see the future you seek. I will charge you no more for this. Come, it is safe."

Why had she not taken my hand? Surely she did not detect the lack of pulse when I wore so encompassing an illusion. I followed her. What did she see? The evening began to look quite entertaining.

Inside the low, sugarloaf shaped tent candles sputtered and leaped about demonically. Thick carpets and horsehair pillows filled the central area. The rest lay hidden behind tattered brocade curtains that reflected candlelight and made the interior not so gloomy. There were few chairs and only one small table holding an ewer and several brass goblets.

She reached a slender bare arm behind the curtain and pulled out a leather bag and a ceramic goblet. Into this she poured me watered wine, and poured herself a drink into one of the brass goblets. I asked, "What is your name, dear? You are so beautiful, so…different."

She gazed evenly at me, showing no emotion. After a

moment she said, "You can call me Zanya." Not her true name, but sufficient. Zanya. A world-straddler.

From the bag she unwrapped silk and fur to reveal a perfectly round crystal, a dragon's tear they call it in the far eastern lands.

I gasped. I had only seen one before and it was in my possession. She smiled quickly at my surprise and something, a glint of knowing, showed in her eyes. She held the ball out on the silk cloth and said, "State your questions and gaze into the crystal."

I reached for it. "No," she said. "Do not touch, just look and ask. I shall do the rest."

So I did as she bid. Her heart beat so slowly that I was distracted by its song. But I turned my attention back to the crystal and gazed at it as she did. The guttural laughing and strident boasts of soldiers and wanderers outside faded into the darkness. What had been the hammer and clatter of brass and iron and pottery diluted to a melodic chorus of angels whispering of secrets I was no longer allowed to know. The odorous smell of unwashed bodies, garlic and tripe, and animal waste drifted away and all I smelled was her spicy musk mixed with the smoky elusiveness of the candles.

Momentarily, I forgot who I was. I looked on her in the space out of time and felt my heart beat once. To be human again, to feel the full thrum of all things living coursing through and around me. This one, this unique creature *was* life. She was the center of the vortex, the eye of the storm, and I would rage and howl about her until she was mine. Mine to savor, body and soul. I had been damned too long and knew humanity was but an elusive dream.

I came to myself weeping and quickly wiped away the tears before she saw the blood. I watched her draw back into the world too. She had been a statue but more animate, an angel in suspension. Her body quivered, her heart sped up and her chest rose and fell quickly. Beads of sweat that I wished to lick rolled down her brow. She spoke huskily.

"You have no children and yet you do. They will

betray you, all but one. Beware what you set in motion. It will plague you throughout eternity." She stopped, shuddered and quickly tucked the crystal ball away. She stood rapidly, shaking from head to toe. I reached out to her and she dropped the silver back into my palm.

"Go. I cannot charge you. You are not what you seem. Go."

I rose and left without asking more. A powerful one. But what had frightened her so? I had seen that look before. It is the look of one who realizes her end has arrived and she cannot stop it. It is the look of absolute loss. It is the look of one who has stared into the abyss.

The night was still young and my game had left me with a melancholy. I decided to add some spice. I disappeared for a while, changing again my appearance. Then I re-entered the flow of nighttime thrill seekers and walked up behind the Hun who still stood unmoving.

I whispered in his ear. "One who stands so conspicuously invites the taste of Greek fire. It is a large city, *and* we are at the perimeters, but they are still suspicious of the unusual."

He turned, his sword already out and arcing. So was mine. "Templar," his guttural voice snarled. "Your type has been a thorn in my side long enough."

Good. Quick to anger. I laughed at him, sheathed my sword and jumped quickly out of the way of his sword.

He stopped. Slowly he sheathed his sword, squinting, then tilted his head as if listening. "I should have suspected. None human can sneak up like that. And who are you?"

I bowed low. "You can call me Dmitri. Welcome to Constantinople, cousin. And have you come to whisper love words in the ears of our emperor? He is hard pressed to help those in such states as your domain when his own is failing. Or is it that you wish to have the Church's devout followers help you squelch the Templars' barrage, as well as those mangy dogs who are howling at your heels?"

He growled, "I have no time for your word games. I

have other prey to hunt."

I motioned away from the small crowd that had gathered, expecting to see some blood spray. "Unless you're looking for a meal, come away. Too much attention is only good if you plan to perform. Once away I will change to something that offends you less."

He growled, "If you want to talk, go change and come back. I enjoy watching these bloodbags. And I care little what they think."

It would not be easy to divert his attention. "Fine. I shall return, but let us meet under that brewer's awning. It is more amenable to conversation, Voivode Stanislaw." His head came up quickly, like a wild beast smelling its prey. "You are the great Stanislaw, are you not?"

His hands opened and closed at his hips. "What makes you think—"

"With so much strife in your homelands, it is a wonder to see anyone here at all. Only the most powerful, and one not involved in immediate conflict, would venture to leave his fiefdoms at such a time. You risk much here."

"Then you would do well to stay away from me lest you be drawn into my fate." He turned away and continued to watch the crowd.

I shrugged and disappeared, to return moments later in my near normal guise. I still wore a thin illusion of a darker, shorter man to others but I had no doubt that Stanislaw saw through this illusion.

I had hoped that he had moved on, but he had only moved enough to lean back against a post that supported a large awning, rolled up for the night to let the moon gleam down on the dark streets. Pan's wild power coursed toward the heart of the city. Great games would ensue before I saw the moon to her bed.

Just then the Ascingani prepared for their evening's entertainment. Zanya emerged from her tent. She strode with purpose, head high; none of her earlier fear showed. She walked up to a withered parchment of a woman and to a tall man of middle age with a great long beard and mustache. She spoke quickly to them, motioning into the crowd. The old woman shook her head and reached into a pouch at her side, while the man moved back a pace from Zanya and held out his hand. He spoke stridently, leaning forward, pointing to the tents. Zanya stomped her foot and waved her arms about until the man shouted at her.

Voivode Stanislaw noticed the altercation. He pushed away from the pole, coming alive it seemed, as if for the first time. I quickly wove through the gathering crowd to reach his side.

"You're just in time for the bear dancing," I said lightly. He ignored me. So, he knew who I was. "I see there is something else that intrigues you."

His hands clenched again at his sides and he licked his lips. "Yes. So...different. I've never seen one like that before."

"Like what?" I asked softly for.

"Her spirit—aura. Such an odd mix."

I saw the Ascingani man point again to the tent. Zanya left but said a few words first. The old woman pulled a long wrap tighter about herself and whispered up at the man. Then she grew silent and rocked to herself. The man walked toward another tent, his shoulders sagging, and picked up a great urn full of wine.

Another man came out with the bear on its length of iron chain. Musicians gathered and the dance began. Over the clamor I asked Stanislaw, "And what does her spirit tell you?"

"She is strong and uses magic. But she is suspicious and afraid. Perhaps an innocent mage? Delightful." He laughed a deep belly laugh that would have been pleasant coming from most men. "*That* will be something to savor."

I'd been afraid of that. He sought my morsel. While I contemplated the problem the ursine moved ponderously. I returned to my senses when the bear howled in pain.

It reared up on its hind legs and swayed, shaking its

head and pawing at it as if a thousand bees stung it. Whiffing, it fell back to all fours, then rolled and leaped about biting at its haunches. Stanislaw. Some of us can talk to animals; others only torture them by being in their minds.

Zanya ran out of the tent as the man tried to control the bear. Stanislaw moved closer and I got stuck in the crowd. I exerted my strength and pushed people out of the way. The crowd grew restless, fearing the bear's escape. Zanya tried to calm it. She moved her hands, working thaumaturgy as the old woman tossed powder from her pouch onto the ursine. Slim, dark Zanya had fire in her eyes. She glared into the crowd looking for the perpetrator.

Her gaze slid over my face then came back to me. She looked past and her glare locked Stanislaw. She faltered in her incantation, her hands momentarily frozen into claws, and her skin paling under her dark complexion.

He grinned and licked his lips and moved closer. I reached out and grasped his arm. "She is under my protection. Choose another."

He turned toward me, enraged, his teeth grinding. "Then you have done a poor job of it."

He grasped my other arm in his crushing grip. I had to move fast or risk a maiming. The crowd watched the bear and did not see me change or strengthen my illusion.

An exquisitely beautiful maiden in a man's tunic now squirmed in his grasp and cried, "Foul fiend, foul fiend, you took my little sister and now you try to rape me. No, no. NO!"

Outraged, he punched at me. I squirmed from his grasp and kicked his shins. Mortals never pierce these delightful illusions, and before the great Voivode knew it he was being pummeled and carried away in a mob of fighting and fury. He would have wounds to lick this night. And I, I would have to walk carefully in the shadows now.

I'm an early riser and the next night I moved quickly to the

Ascingani camp. There was no sign yet of Voivode Stanislaw and perhaps he attended diplomatic matters in the city's heart. I kept an eye out for henchmen, for I was sure he had them lurking nearby.

I found that exquisite rare flower sitting near her encampment, drinking alone in a tavern made of posts and splotchy awnings of indeterminate color. Not many women frequented the tents even in this quarter but those that did received company. No one sat near her. In fact, they stood in clusters enjoying one another's company and sending cautious glances in her direction. She had obviously established her preference long before this night.

I strummed my way through the crowd, singing songs of battle and conquerors and of women aplenty. I know well how to make the coin spill into my palms. Eventually I moved closer, then sat at her table and called for an ale. She did not look up. The server plunked the battered tankard in front of me and went on her way.

I studied her closely, hoping to pick up more about who she was. She stared at the table, a black substance ringing her eyes, and her cheeks bore dots and swirls in some sort of pattern. A tattoo, of course, but I had not seen many wear them outside of the Pictish lands. Her hands were slim, fine-boned like a bird's, and her nails, broken and gritted with dirt. She was young, this world straddler, but of an age when most women were already married. Yet, I knew she was not.

I strummed my lute and sang a bar or two. She looked up suddenly, into my eyes and stilled. Her eyes narrowed slightly but she did not look away. "Good evening, my lady."

She nodded. "I've seen you."

"And hopefully appreciated my song. You are of the Ascingani, yes?"

Her motions were slow, studied and with a tenseness that spoke of an animal trying to evade a trap. She nodded again and sipped her wine.

"I have traveled far, as many a minstrel must to play and to gather stories, but I have never seen your people before. Where do you hail from?"

"From here," she motioned about her. "Our home is where we are. Before this, they say we came from Aegypt, and many call us Aegypters."

Many call us. So, a half-truth. "But do you not call yourselves the Rom?"

She twitched, but otherwise betrayed nothing. "There is something about you..."

Best to steer her away. "Will your people bring out the bear to dance tonight? I have rarely seen such skill in training the ursines."

She did not answer but looked out the tent, then drained her cup. "No, the bear rests tonight. I must go. I will dance soon." She rose from the table.

I raised my cup to her. "Then I shall come and watch art made into life."

The compliment startled her. She stopped and looked back at me, then left without a word. Close-mouthed, skilled in telling half-truths. I wondered if all her people were so.

I walked the perimeters, working the crowd. There was as yet no sign of Voivode Stanislaw. There would be though. I found a couple of Rom men pushing barrels along and stopped to help them. After a short conversation I knew that they were all like Zanya, adept at secrets and reading others. I would be well tested against these mortals.

I chose a spot not blocked by tents or shops that overlooked the Rom encampment. People drifted by pulling mantles tight against the evening breeze. I blended away into shadows and sat down to wait. If Stanislaw looked, he would find me. Otherwise, someone who does not breathe, or radiate warmth or heartbeat passes well as stone.

I became as stone in my thoughts, drifting back to my youth when I had been part of a small sect who kept the capricious god Pan alive in our hearts. Even then the fairly new Christian god did not inspire me. There was not the fiery passion and wild abandon to ecstasy and ritual that had fired the Greek pantheon. I had been to Eleusis and performed the rites. Even in my youth they had diminished to pales shades of their former glory but I had felt the divine spark of Demeter and her daughter Persephone touch me in those rites. And so I worshipped Pan, his ardor, his wild ways, his lust, his music. And Pan, always unpredictable, had touched me. It was more Persephone though, queen of the underworld, or one much like her who had forever altered my world. I had cursed Pan wholly for my fall, but then in the end had found solace in the gods, and so I did their bidding. And still I followed Pan.

Diverse entertainment came and went while I mused. When the music started I directed my attention to the torchlit enclosure and watched as Zanya leaped into the center to loud drums and horns. She was not a flower opening slowly, or the dance of joyful butterflies. No, she was the fire, the molten core of the earth erupting and flaring about. She was the source of life, suddenly released from its fleshy cage and singeing everyone's souls. Her hair writhed in firelight like Medusa's head of snakes. Her arms undulated and her feet stamped and kicked, churning up the dormant lives about her.

Again I was touched to my cold dead soul, and again I yearned to have her. With a jolt that almost made me drop my illusion, I realized I was nearly in love with this creature. That had not been part of the game. It was a dangerous fault and had not happened in a very long time. I wondered if I had clouded my perceptions. Then I saw Stanislaw in the shadows, watching Zanya.

The crowd dispersed when she finished. The Ascingani began putting away their instruments and closing up the tents. Zanya talked with the man of the night before, as animated as she had been while dancing. Her skin gleamed gold under sweat and firelight. What she argued, I know not, for the words were in an unknown language. Again it was as if the man refused her and she stormed away to a water barrel and pulled a ladle from it. The barrel was close to where I waited. A mixture of despair and resignation crossed her features before she drank.

She whirled as Stanislaw approached, though no human could have heard his step. She knew and faced him, then cried in a language I understood, "You! What do you want?"

Stanislaw did not answer but reached out to her and touched her cheek. She screamed, a sound not of physical pain but of something deeper, more injured. Quickly she made a sigil in the air, her fingers dancing agilely as she chanted something guttural. Stanislaw grunted and pulled back his hand. There was a long gash in it.

"*Mulo*," she hissed. "*Shilmulo! Kumpania!* Kavi, Bardo—"

The rest was lost in shouts and her cry. She quickly grabbed a torch as Stanislaw advanced, his fangs distended, ready for the kill. Zanya backed up. She thrust the torch at him and he stepped back. Then her people were about her, with torches and long blades.

Stanislaw held his arm in front of his face. He growled and fled.

I approached while they were unaware and said, "Can I be of help?"

A burly man glanced at me, squinted and muttered, "It is no concern of yours, *gadjo*. The matter is done."

Zanya said something to him and he grunted, but left with the others. I walked with her to her tent. "I'm sorry," I blustered. "I would have come to your aid earlier but I was too far away from that...man. What is it you called him?"

She stopped and looked at me, her tawny eyes piercing into my inner being. I was sure she read my mind. Could she? "There is something about you..."

I bowed, exuding confidence and a quick smile. "Dmitri at your service, lady."

She was not so easily won. "You are different. Our

fates are linked. I like it not."

"What is a *shilmulo*, what you called him?"

She folded her arms as if to keep the chill from her body. She seemed to weigh the answer before she spoke. "Someone who is dead, a ghost. A *dhampyr*, one that sucks the blood from the living. We wish it on no man." She shuddered, looking hollow-eyed.

Curious, I asked, "But how could you tell that by—"

She sniffed and turned her head away. "Among your kind you have mages, have you not? Alchemists, those who mix the worlds we cannot see. I am *chovihani* to my people. I see more than with the eyes, enough that my own people are wary of me."

"Is that why I saw you arguing earlier?"

"I wish to leave before it is too late. Before the other world—" She twitched as if she had not realized I was still there. Not meeting my eyes, she said, "I thank you for your goodwill. Good evening." She entered the tent's dark embrace.

Suffice to say, Stanislaw did not find me. Sometimes my games escape me, swerve from the path and leave me searching, not knowing which course they took.

I spent half the night looking for Stanislaw's crypt, thinking he would not make his move too early on the Rom camp armed as they were with charms. I wandered through winding refuse-laden alleys, past alehouses spilling drunken vermin and through dark shrouded homes slumbering against the evils of the city. Few approached me, but I batted all away, unheeding of their desires. I risked much but I did not lose my head. Finally, with no success, I returned to the Rom camp, illusion still covering me from their bright eyes.

I exhaled with relief. The camp was quiet, having already thrown itself into the welcoming arms of sleep. Or almost all of them. I heard a strangled whimper and followed the thread of its sound.

There was little noise. Only a faint rustle and the soft bubbling sound of someone drinking, no—slurping at something thick. I knew before I lifted the flap what I would see. As I stepped into the near darkness of Zanya's tent I saw the old woman huddled near the opening. She who had thrown powder upon the maddened ursine was now beyond movement. A gash opened her throat in a silent scream. On the carpet of pillows and furs, I saw Stanislaw, still robed in his furs and wool, though a long gash from chin to navel bloodied his clothes.

He held the bedraggled head of some thing to his chest. It slurped at his wound. Only the long tangled hair and the amber skin told me it was Zanya. She had put up a fight. So had the old woman from the signs of spilled lanterns and ripped clothing, but it is hard to beat one as strong as Stanislaw.

"I said she was under my protection."

Stanislaw looked up, black eyes glinting in the single candle's light. He barked once. "And I said you were a poor protector. She has been drained and now begins to drink, and will be mine forever more. Not quite dead; quite a horror to these bloodbags."

"No!" I saw life's ember being extinguished, something so vital did not deserve this death—or life. She had been mine, for my ends. He took not only her, but from me, for spite, for malice, for his own twisted pleasure. I would curse later for leaving too much up to Pan's whim. As it was, I cursed him, and myself for slowness. "NO! You will leave her."

I grabbed one of the poles that served to keep the tent flaps open in the heat of day and snapped it in my bare hands. I charged him, hoping to pierce his black heart before he finished. A moment before I struck Stanislaw twitched to the left and I pierced his right chest instead of the left. He roared and rose to his feet, reaching out to grab my wrist.

I threw a brazier of fire in his face. He flung up his arms to ward off the flames. His skin smoked. Losing blood, he lurched from the tent, cradling his right arm. He was far from finished. I heard him cry out in his harsh tongue. I was sure his minions had carted him away.

I looked at Zanya as she lay near death on her bed. She had been too bright, a life so shining I would have watched her for an age. Now, I pulled back my linen sleeve and dragged my nail through my own flesh. Before I realized what I did I held her mouth to my wound and let her fill the rest of her need with my blood. I realized then that dawn approached and though I could withstand a quick run through the encroaching light, she was vulnerable. I would not leave her here.

I heard them now. Alarm filled their voices. I pulled my arm away from her hungry lips. "Enough, though I dare say you won't thank me. We must be away."

I pulled her to her feet, then threw her over my shoulder and ran. There were catacombs close to the city walls and I had long since known the entrance. I quickly made for them as the sun topped the shaggy mounds of stalls and tents.

Already the unlife took its hold upon the Rom woman. She began to shake and twitch. When we were far enough into the cool stone womb I pushed crumbling bones off of a slab and laid her out. As she groaned and spasmed, whispering in her own language, I grabbed her head in my hands.

"Look at me. Zanya, look." Her eyes, unfocused by pain, flitted over my gaze then came back, though her body still shivered and twisted under my grasp. "You are not dead, nor do you live. You are, as you say, now *shilmulo*. You will not thank me for this. Aye, you may well hate me but I have saved you from a worse existence of slavery. Now you will experience great pain, then a lassitude and awake to pain. There is naught else I can do at the moment but kill you, and that I do not wish."

I saw the utter fear in her eyes, just as when she had read the crystal. This then had been her foreboding. Her body curled in on itself and her head twitched to the side as she disgorged her last mortal meal.

I spent an hour with her, maybe two as her body grew accustomed to its new role. I cursed Pan all the while. The gods indeed were capricious and I had surely killed her as much as Stanislaw. All gods look with a heedless eye upon our deeds. We caper freely, therefore condemning ourselves farther to hell, or purgatory, or Hades—it matters little the name.

I had to wonder what strange fruit I nurtured here. A world-straddler to begin with. This was not the fate I had wanted, was it? I had wanted to taste her, not consume her, but my game had gotten out of hand. Stanislaw had played his own game.

I subsided into a fitful lethargy as she did, sleeping through the lightest hours of the day. I'm an early riser, but I was surprised to wake to Zanya's fitful curses, as she whimper but did not weep. That she was still wracked with the pains of change, there was no doubt.

She moaned, then saw me. "What am I? What have you made me?"

I shrugged and smiled, staring up at her on the stone pallet where she hunched like a mountain cat waiting to spring. "Like you said, a *dhampyr*. Damned, if you prefer." I rose and brushed back my hair. I usually had better chambers to recline in. "Come," I held out my hand. "I will tell you what I can while we walk."

She scrambled back on the palette and jumped off, backing away from me. "You! You were the old woman. Your fate and mine..."

I bowed. "And as the great god Pan wishes."

"I will seek my own way!"

"Do you know of the sun's burning kiss, the lingering touch of a stake, the hunger that will consume you as it rages within?"

She gathered dirty cloth into her hands, crushing it to her breast and wailed, "Do you know what I have lost? The touch of animals, the view of the future, the thread that ties me to all else? My soul?! My people? My blood? You have taken everything!"

She ran then, out into the night. I sighed. I am not so cruel or bestial that I would leave her to the fates. I followed. She entered near the lowliest merchant stalls that sold used rags and iron. As she fled a horse on the main road nearly ran her down. The horse reared.

I stopped to the side as the rider swung down. He grabbed her arm. I saw the saturnine face of Stanislaw. His horse was saddled with bags, and his retinue hung back a few paces, watching hungrily, sniffing the air like dogs.

"You," he growled, then looked at me. "You. I should have suspected games."

"And I should have expected nightmares."

Zanya wrenched her arm free and danced out of his range. She spit in his face and then raised an arm to point at him. "I curse you both with the power of the Rom, with the bloodline that has flowed through me for generations, while there is any blood left in me. You will rue the day you abused my kind and me. You have made me untouchable, it is the worst fate. Know this, I will pursue you till the end of time, and you have given me means. If I do not, then those that come after me, who follow my cause, shall pursue you. We will fill your lands, your home, everywhere that you turn; we will be there and we will seek out you and yours and destroy you. Only then, will I release myself from this hateful...being!"

She added words in her Rom tongue and spat again, accurately hitting his face. "And you," she turned toward me. "Better to have killed me. You will never be free of me or mine either. For all your days we shall follow you and watch you and yours. We will be everywhere in every land and if you foul us or go against us we will destroy you too. I swear this, by all my ancestors before and after, that I will track you both till the end of your days."

At that she turned and fled. Stanislaw stood still. Was

he in shock? I myself felt a momentary shiver course down my spine. I knew she had the power, if she survived, to carry out her curse. I turned to follow her but Stanislaw barked out, "You are not welcome in my lands. If it was not that I have been called away I would hunt you and that other down now and drain you both of tainted blood."

With that he mounted his shying horse and galloped down the road. I stood on the outskirts of Constantinople wondering again about its strange fruits and the flavors that colored the night air. I shrugged again and murmured, "Pan." This was a game that I would be a long time in playing, trying to set the pieces aright. I wondered if I had gambled too much.

IT'S ONLY WORDS

When Lloyd left his apartment, miserable hit him like a tsunami. It was bad enough he'd lost his hat the day before, his umbrella was at the office and that the weather was the worst temper tantrum nature had thrown in five years. But to add to the insult that the world was heaping on him was a tow truck pulling away with his car hitched to it like a reluctant lover.

"H-h-ha... Hey!" He ran after the truck, waving frantically, frigid rain lancing his face.

His frantic action caught the driver's attention and he pulled to a halt. Casually he rolled down the window and regarded Lloyd, a toothpick stuck between his lips.

"M-m-mah m-my c-c-ca-car." He yelled over the noise.

"Yeah?" The guy smirked at him, his toothpick twitching. "Well you can get it for the Hasty Tow lot on Kent St."

Lloyd shook his head. "Wh-wh…" He stopped, chewing the inside of his cheek. The words would not come, never came easily, always reluctant to leave the warm cavern of his mouth. Always smothered by the noise. "Wh-whu-whu-why?"

The driver's brown eyebrows went up. He passed Lloyd the ticket. "No permit."

Lloyd gave up trying to relay his thoughts and instead held up his finger and pulled out his car keys. Rain trickled into his eyes and dripped off the end of his nose as if he were a waterspout. He ran to the car and jiggled the key in the lock, popping the door before the tow truck driver could say anything. He looked in the interior strewn with cups and food wrappers, and sure enough, there was the permit, having slipped down on the seat.

Brandishing it like the winning lottery ticket, Lloyd shoved it at the man, who just shrugged. "Too bad man, it wasn't where it was supposed to be. Take it up with the courts."

Something contracted, then blew apart within Lloyd. His vision went black, hazing to gray. Enraged, he clenched his fists. Treated yet again like an ineffectual pimple on humanity's butt. Everyone making fun of him for his stutter. People playing games for their own power. He hadn't just had enough. It was time to turn the tables, time to let them know what he thought. Time to get the words out.

His vision compressed to a pinpoint of searing light. It was as if his essence became a concentrated seed of intent with the density of a black hole. Slashing water out of his eyes, he glared at the driver and pulled his wallet from his sodden pants. He held it up. "Mu-muh-muh-muh-money." No. He concentrated, temporarily choking out the noise. "I have money…at the house."

The guy grinned like it was the only thing that mattered. "It will cost you a hundred bucks, cheaper than the impound."

Lloyd just nodded, listening to the hidden laughter. Far cheaper, but not for this arrogant sack of flesh. He waited until the driver backed his car into its spot and lowered it to the pavement. Then Lloyd beelined to his door, opened it and grabbed the cast iron cockroach that served as a doorstop. By the time the driver sauntered up the steps Lloyd flourished the five twenties like a bouquet.

As the guy took them and audaciously counted the bills Lloyd conked him over the head. He had to repeat the action, then step over the driver to lock the door. He'd show him. Lloyd particularly hated the good-looking people who treated him like they were better. It didn't matter that the guy had a lackluster job; he still felt superior. Lloyd would fix that but not now.

Dragging the unconscious man into the den, he hogtied his arms and legs with thick red rope, then gagged him with a sturdy rag. The man looked pretty fit so Lloyd tied the ropes to the unused weight set on one wall and the support pillar on the other. Last, he checked the pockets and removed the cellphone and keys, tossing them in the hallway on his way out.

Work passed in automatic mode. Talking was rarely required between filing the insurance adjustors' paperwork and the email to various clients. Lloyd's hands worked on their own, like army ants, and his mind raced and spun, pulsed and dove to the core of his problem. He would get respect. He would tell his tale, any way he could. They would listen.

There was never any moment that Lloyd was alone, even living by himself. The constant companionship, the incessant susurrus of voices filled his head. *They* could speak, *they* told their stories but he never had been able to shout above the crowd. They never let him be heard. It was his turn, and people would know his story.

Driving back to his home, he only stopped to pick up some food; a bag of green beans, onions and chicken. And then to the local Wal-Mart to get some sweat pants and a T-shirt. Luckily it was Friday and he could complete his project in peace. Relative peace that was, with only the unseen that always kept him company.

He parked across the street, noticing the tow truck still sitting at the corner. No one ever towed a tow truck. That didn't matter; not right now.

Inside he listened for a moment and heard muffled thumping. Peeking inside the den, he saw the driver was pretty much where Lloyd had left him. And he was awake. When he saw Lloyd he struggled harder, his face turning red and veins like well-fed worms standing out on his neck and face. Although he tried to speak his words were smothered by the gag and Lloyd smiled. Now he had a taste of what Lloyd's world was like.

Lloyd shut the door and prepared supper, humming to himself, trying to quell the chittering and laughter in his head. If the voices had ever carried on intelligent dialogue Lloyd might not have minded. But they kept him isolated in a cage of sound, random words, hissing, laughter, growls, so he could barely ever hear what he was saying.

After dinner, still humming, Lloyd gathered his tools; a silver bowl full of paste, scissors, and then he entered the den. The first thing he did was remove the man's socks, boots and belt. As he began cutting off the jeans and shirt, the man whimpered and tried to squirm away.

"Shh, shh," was all Lloyd said.

When the driver lay naked on the floor, really just a man with no sign of status or occupation, Lloyd couldn't help but smile seeing that the guy didn't have a very large cock, especially lying limp against his leg.

The voices grew loud, a crowd looking in, wondering what Lloyd was up to. He ran into the bathroom gasping, clutching at his head. In the mirror he looked ordinary enough, hard cheekbones, a few lines about his mouth, triangular head topped with black swirls of hair. Black as ink on flesh as white as paper. He squeezed his temples, trying to expunge the voices in his head. The hairs on his body were like fine lines of text but nobody had ever been able to read what was written. How could he make people understand? How could he join the jostle of humanity and leave the echoing sounds that kept him in his head?

He'd seen *The Cook, the Thief, His Wife and Her Lover* where the lover had been crammed with pages of a book, like a lamb stuffed with grape leaves. Like a lamb to the slaughter. Slaughter and laughter had no place in a sentence together but it was sentences he hoped for, words to swallow the demonic laughter that ricocheted off the inside of his head, ringing and clanging and filling his thoughts with an awful echoing din.

Lloyd clenched his fists and took two deep breaths, then grabbed a jar from under the sink and walked back to the bound man. Without touching him, he slipped the jar over the man's flaccid penis. "G-gu-go."

The man shook his head, his eyes wide and sweaty hair plastered to his brow. The room smelled of oniony sweat but Lloyd didn't mind. He repeated the request, keeping the jar in place until the man closed his eyes and pissed into the jar. A tear trickled out of one eye. When he was done, Lloyd emptied the contents and returned to the den.

He ignored his prisoner and looked upon the shelves upon shelves of books that walled the den. Which would best tell his story? His was not a tale of romance or whimsy, nor one of humor and science. His was a chronicle of pain and loneliness, terror and chaos.

He pulled the *Horror Library* volumes off the shelves, and *Cone Zero, Picking Up the Ghost*, which made him giggle (he was a living ghost), the *Evolve* anthology on vampires and at least six other books. He didn't need them anymore. The words were in him after all and the tales were deep and disturbing. Lloyd had begun to read horror as a teenager when the voices grew too loud. The terrible stories made him feel better, helped him continue for there were worse fates out there. But sometimes he had really wondered.

He took his time, leafing through the pages to find the right passages and cutting them out of each book. As he did so, he ran the strip of paper through the paste and laid it on the man's body, smoothing it down like wallpaper. Though the man struggled at first, he subsided to Lloyd's ministrations.

Lloyd worked tirelessly through the night, humming and cutting and pasting. Sometimes he could cut out whole sentences, like, "I felt like weeping; not crying, weeping." Or "There seemed to be a dozen random thoughts trying to break out all at once." But more often, even with horror books he still had to piece sentences together from individual words. In a way, it was much like trying to get out a sentence verbally but this way he could complete his dark tale. The laborious and tedious process would still be worth it.

Lloyd stopped for sips of water to wash the cacophony down his throat, cool his thoughts. Late into the night when the man's torso was covered front and back and only the legs remained, Lloyd undid the gag and gave the man some water. He untied the ankles but left the hands bound to opposite sides. The man lay still, splayed on his back, covered with words and sentences, a library of Lloyd's dialogue. An open book. But though he was weighted with the text he still hadn't heard. Not yet.

It was around noon when Lloyd finished the patchwork man, covered from the bottoms of his feet, all up his torso, even along his cheeks and nose. His eyes were open and calm, staring. Humming, Lloyd took the last strip of text but did not dip it in paste. Reverently he laid it across his tongue, feeling the buzz and murmur of the voices. There was a curiosity to their hiss and hum. Bending over the spread-eagled, print-imbued man, Lloyd pried his mouth open and slowly touched his tongue to the other's.

For the first time since he was a young boy there was utter stillness about him. The absence of voices and laughter left him with a sphere of possibility. He heard his heart and the other man's heart beating erratically. Their breath was not in sync and it was loud, the furnace turned on within the depths of the house and dust motes floated down. But it was so blessed quiet that Lloyd gasped and shivered with delight.

Then the paper slid off of his tongue and onto the man's tongue. With their mouths still open, touching tongue to tongue, the voices screamed out of Lloyd, thrashing into the man until his body convulsed and quivered. Roaring, the sound left him; laughter, maniacal and terrifying rippled over the man. Within seconds all the sound had rushed out and Lloyd collapsed beside the comatose man.

Minutes passed and Lloyd pushed himself up, looking down at the man beside him. "Now you have my story." The man's flesh showed no signs of text except for the very lightest shadowing that no one would notice unless looking closely. Lloyd untied him and sat him up like a rag doll, pulling on pants and T-shirt, socks and then boots. When the man came to he looked over at Lloyd and tilted his head. Lloyd helped him to his feet and gave him his cell and keys.

At the door, the guy started muttering. Lloyd leaned in but couldn't hear all that he said. Random words. Perhaps it would take time for his story to sink in. He gently pushed the man out the door, saying "Take it easy." The police never showed up so he was sure his message had been heard.

The quiet lasted a week, like a blanket of melting snow, and then the voices began to trickle back. Lloyd lay in his bed whimpering with frustration. Not again, not after all he had suffered. He squeezed his hands into fists and pressed them against his eyes. He would not stay the victim. Now that he knew how to speak, he would address the world. There were many people to be taught a lesson in stories; those who needed to consider others. It would help them he knew, bringing balance. After all, the pen was purported to be mightier than the sword and he did not harm the people. They would go on to understand that even the voiceless deserved to be heard.

The next was a haughty and beautiful woman who snapped at him in the parking lot. Lloyd found an easier way with ether because he was too afraid of giving brain damage with knocking people over the head. But he bound her just the same. Thinking women were the weaker sex had been many a villain's downfall in the books. Though he undressed her and pasted strips of text over her body like a literary mummy he did not take advantage of her. Admittedly he lapped her body with his eyes, and his hands quivered when he placed the strips over her breasts and pubic area. But to do more than impart his tales would have made Lloyd no better than those he tried to rebalance.

The woman too, left like an automaton, muttering under her breath. He was sure he caught phrases he had pasted across her body that had been absorbed into her flesh when the wall of sound had left him.

But again, after a week and a half, Lloyd's world began to fill with a cacophony on whisperings and maniacal laughter. It was almost worse to have the sound return after experiencing the quietude of the mind that most people took for granted. Lloyd wept but his tears did not wash away the noise. The flood stayed within him.

He pulled more volumes off of his shelf, stripping away and disposing of the covers. *Tattered Souls* was an apt title for the way he felt. He used up the *Evolve* anthology first, finished off the first two volumes of *Horror Library* and started in on *Cern Zoo*. The printed words served him well for his third and fourth students. Any fiction books might have done in the long run but Lloyd used what he had and continued to make people into living books, the story of his life, his fears and his isolation. They always looked like mummies before he held the last sentence on his tongue and transferred it to their mouths.

Months passed and Lloyd continued to try and bring balance into his life and therefore to those who were arrogant or cruel, selfish or inconsiderate. No matter how many people he papered the well of sounds only ran dry for two weeks, a short reprieve from the mad songs that curdled his own words. He always had a few days of normal dialogue that they began to notice at work, and which he explained as therapy.

But it never lasted. The inner madness returned again and again, shuttering Lloyd in as he clutched at his head. He'd learned long ago that alcohol only increased the voices. Nothing removed them but the papering of others. He wept, and continued his ministry of tale transference. Surely there would be a point when enough people would know him and understand him and he would not be alone. Alone like he was now, with laugher and whisperings his faithful yet unwanted companions.

A year later, time having moved along in fits and starts, Lloyd walked through the city's more impoverished area, past pale buildings where paint peeled like old skin, and houses that slouched on their foundations. Yards held broken bikes and swings, derelict cars, old papers, moldering couches. The day was clear and cool and yet the street was empty so he moved into the more middle class area. Here the shops were nondescript but clean, lacking originality and people moved in and out of stores like ants. The windows sported the latest sales but otherwise stared blankly back at him.

Perhaps a different class of person would quell the voices longer, but Lloyd knew this untrue as he had already used men and women, young and old, rich and poor, and none had yet taken his story completely. If they had truly acknowledged him then his inner world would have been silence instead of chattering demons. He had been sure it had worked and it had, but for short periods. As he strolled along the street, lost in thoughts that were becoming crowded by the incessant whispering, he noticed that a person here or there wandered aimlessly, dressed poorly, looking blank and nearly mad. One young man passed him and he heard the muttering voice.

A woman, better dressed, quite pretty actually, walked by. Straining, Lloyd heard her.

"Dark matter…song…lonely…hssss…shhhh….gob…miss me." Then she laughed and continued, muttering as she walked.

Lloyd stopped and stared after her, noticing here and there, other people doing the same. Some looked more lucid. He ran up to one and grabbed the man's chin, making him look up. "Ssstttot calypso…meow…clip…tongue lash…Freon." They didn't even speak in sentences, just random words.

He checked another but it was the same. Some people looked calm, others seemed desperate and maddened. But everyone's lips moved and he knew nonsense spewed from them. Lloyd turned a slow circle, hearing the echoes and cries in his own head and looked up and down the street. With realization washing over him like an incoming tide, he knew that some of these people were the ones he had marked with his tales. Maybe all of them. He had given them the story of his life, told his saga of woes and loneliness so that they would understand and come to be more compassionate beings.

But that is not what he saw. There were people chatting to friends and busying themselves in shopping, who stopped to smell an orange. He saw normal life, people who could think and relate their thoughts and feelings to each other easily. There was love and family and friendship. But the man in the wool jacket and jeans, the woman in the pretty green dress, the man just staring into the street—all of those people didn't interact. Instead their lips moved and they moved, walled within the sound in their own heads.

A flush of heat took Lloyd and his heart contracted. He had given people his story, letting out words so that he would be part of the human community. But it had not been as he thought. They had only heard the tale for a short time before being overcome. No one had made him their friend.

With a sick hollowness filling him, Lloyd realized he was the wellspring. From him had come his tale but it had been infected. He had not told people how he felt so that they could remember. He had not expunged the mad murmurings from his own mind but had only spread the disease throughout other people. He had thought it only words he passed on, but it had been a plague he had spread to humanity.

EXEGESIS OF THE INSECTA APOCRYPHA

In the beginning, it was a shift, a flutter of orange and black that caught her eye and held it, pulling her into a new paradigm before she knew there ever was one. The opening of the butterfly's wings fastened her two-year-old gaze forever." *Apocryphon I*[1]

The Apocrypha *first appeared on the World Wide Web in the early twenty-first century. Their legitimacy as sacred writing was not considered for two decades, with arguments reiterating that class Insecta could never evolve to the state of written language, let alone into a mindset able to formulate histories and concepts of time. In light of the documented case of the child with compound eyes being born last year, as well as several climatic shifts that have increased insect populations, the* Insecta Apocrypha *are being analyzed for new interpretations. Whether they are indicators of a convergence of evolution and intelligence to a new level is not in the purview of this paper.*

What draws the eye immediately is the symbolism. Butterflies and birds have long been seen as forms of the human soul. Just as the Bible opens with Genesis, so does the Apocrypha begin with a genesis of sorts, and at the awakening of a child's consciousness begins the search for the meaning of soul.[2]

APOCRYPHON I–DISCOVERY

Ever since that first erratic flight, Libby's gaze followed minute forms of locomotion. Whether a larva wriggling, a beetle scuttling, a dragonfly flitting and hovering, or the leap of a grasshopper, she watched intently, tracing its path as long as possible. At the age of four, she squatted in the garden, staring intently at something that shivered the long grass. Inhaling noisily, she wrinkled her nose at the cloying smell but stayed put.

Her father's words were less than a fly's buzz and her chubby little fingers itched to pick up one of the writhing white maggots that worked its way in and out of what was once a mouse. The gray brown fur was nearly indistinguishable under the moving carpet that gently trembled.

In that instant Libby understood that life was cannibalistic, feeding on itself, but taking different forms. Life fed on death, death generated life—an intrinsic cycle.

Early on, she noticed that people shied from answering her questions about death and decay. It disturbed them, especially when insects were involved in the decomposition. There was something about the mindless infestation of life feeding voraciously on the dead. A need was deposited in her, a small egg incubating, maturing the more attention she gave it, until it could eat its way out of her. The larval thought was curiosity, but it was inherently tied to watching life and death.

Her father buried the mouse and its white pulsing attendants, digging a hole so deep that Libby never found the spot again.

One humid morning brought mosquitoes swarming from the creek in the back field. Libby had been walking with her mother, who had stopped to take a few pictures of plants. She listened to the whine of mosquitoes and held out her arm. They alighted, a half dozen or so, their needle thin proboscises piercing her flesh. They sucked and fattened on her blood. Although it itched slightly, Libby didn't interfere with their feeding until her mother turned and said, "Libby, what are you doing!"

Her mother frantically brushed the mosquitoes from her arm and dragged Libby out of the woods, swatting the whole time. At home Libby found her arm swathed in calamine. She watched it throughout the next day, fascinated by the reddish bumps that arose. If she scratched them long enough they enlarged and seeped a clear liquid before blood oozed like small volcanoes erupting. She licked her wounds, feeling the heat of her skin and the slight sourness of the scabs.

She never shied from any insect, letting red-backed ladybirds and butterflies alight on her, moving her feet into the path of shiny, black carapaced June bugs, or walking into a spider's web to induce the arachnid to crawl across her. Holding her mouth open, she would stick out her tongue, letting a few brave insects land so that she could feel the soft dance of their feet. Bites and stings often laced her skin and left her parents bewildered.

Children have a natural curiosity and, like cats, they will watch anything that moves. They are sometimes considered cruel when, in their discoveries, they tear apart insects or hit another child with a stick. Libby's early experiences, when read without the fictional embellishments, are within the normal range of a child's development and expanding consciousness.

It is possible that this early infusion of insect venoms laid the tracery for Libby's later metamorphosis. Her next stage, in Apocryphon II, *began at the age of six. Libby actively investigated the insect world and was ready to learn the depth of what they could do.*[3]

APOCRYPHON II–EXPERIMENTATION

She found an orange striped kitten in the field behind her house. There was a small stand of alders near the creek and she stood under the fluttering leaves, holding the mewing kitten. Taking a string from her pocket, she tied one end around the cat's neck and the other end around a slender tree. Libby patted the kitten once, then walked away.

It took three days for the insect world and the mammalian one to intersect. Each day she strode quickly to the grove of trees and checked the kitten. The first day it struggled and mewed loudly when it saw her. She turned and left it. The second day, it lay on its side, panting, croaking out a feeble meow. Libby searched for insect activity and on seeing none, left. The third day, she bent over, peering at the prone kitten. Its eyes were open and glassy. The slightly matted fur did not move.

Libby settled herself in the grass, cross-legged, her elbows on her knees, chin in hand. Eventually, she noticed a minuscule flicker. She bent closer and watched fleas, which fed on the living, abandoning the carcass, some leaping off, some disappearing underneath, and even a couple of them crossing the surface of the corpse's blind eyes.

Next, the flies descended, buzzing and settling upon the creature, especially around its eyes, ears and nose. It had died with its mouth slightly open, the pink tongue showing swollen and dark. In crept a fly, glistening blue-black, and another, moving about, probing with insectile feet and mouth. The kitten's body crawled with insects, alighting and flying ellipsoid orbits. Libby removed the string from the cat's neck and returned home by dinnertime so as not to jeopardize her experiment.

Each day, she returned to sit and watch the insect activity. In just a few days, the orange and white fur began to move and ripple, like wind over grass. Glistening maggots tumbled from the mouth and eyes, feeding on necrotic tissue.

Eventually, ants and gnats and beetles crawled over the putrefying mass as the fur sloughed off, displaying the animal's liquefying organs. Libby held vigil through all of it, noting when flies grew bored with the carcass and when ants and spiders moved in to remove morsels. The kitten's body was a motel of activity. Only when the feeding slowed, with mostly bones and fur left, did Libby bury the corpse.

It was a couple of years later that she took a puppy into the same woods. This time she did not wait for death's slow claim but strangled the pup immediately, her hands choking off its whimpers as its black paws scrabbled in the air. When it stopped moving, she laid it on the ground, spreading out its silky ears.

Then she pulled a sharp kitchen knife from her pack. It glinted in the afternoon sun as she studied the black body of the pup. She placed the point against the soft, nearly furless area by the genitals and pushed in, sawing up through the skin to the ribcage. Only a small amount of blackish blood pooled out. Then she cut under the ribs in smaller strokes and across, forming a T. Pulling back the skin and opening the organs to the elements had already brought the flies. Her knife pricked the pink intestines that seeped a fetid black fluid.

Libby sat back as the flies settled upon her offering, humming their contentment. She twirled her wheaten hair, forgetting her hunger and almost missing the distant call of her mother. Scrambling up, Libby tucked away the knife and ran off.

Her diligence brought her each day to note earwigs and the black bowl of Hister beetle backs moving in and out of the architecture of decomposing organs while maggots were born and grew fat on the meat. Within a few days the dog's black skin sloughed off the bloated body. Pupae from the flies eventually cracked their husks, emerging as a new generation.

Libby's interest only grew. Not far from her home was a two-story apartment building slated for demolition.

The vacant shadows of the windows held only shards of glass. Plywood had been nailed up but vagrants and teenagers had pried them away. Libby had already explored the place, seeing what insects lived in dark and dank rooms.

When she was twelve she found a little boy of about five wandering down the street. He seemed to not realize he'd strayed far from the familiar. Libby gave him a cellophane-wrapped candy and as he popped it in his already sticky mouth, she said, "I've lost my puppy. Would you like to help me find him?" The boy nodded, pushing his stringy brown hair out of his eyes but not saying anything around the candy in his mouth. Gummy sweetness streaked his chin with brown and pink.

She took his hand and he followed complacently. It was easy enough to get him into the building and have him sit while she grabbed an old rag and some rope. She deftly tied him and before he could whimper, stuffed the gag in his mouth. He began to cry, soaking the rag with saliva and snot. Libby ignored him while she readied her tools; tweezers and scalpel. A few alert flies already circled the boy's face. From her pack, she withdrew several small jars, each holding a flickering, insectoid mass. In one she had scooped up beetles and earwigs and other ground insects. Another held the agitated buzzing of wasps, while a third showed the constant flutter of color from butterflies and moths. Two more jars contained flies and caterpillars respectively.

She ignored the boy's muffled shrieks, refusing to hurry.

After her experiments, Libby retied the gag on the unconscious boy, most of the insects having abandoned him, and threw a blanket over his body. He would be a better stew in the morning. She left and came back a day later, looking at his welted belly and peering at his crusting arms. Flies buzzed about the trickling snot on his face, landing and walking over his sweat-matted hair.

Libby continued for a couple of days, watching how the fly larvae grew on living tissue. The boy stared vacantly, drooling, barely making a sound. When nothing more could be gained from her observations, she untied him and watched. He didn't move, just lay on his side. Maggots dropped off of his arms. There was no need to kill him. She packed up everything she had brought, removing jars, tweezers, scalpel and rope, leaving nothing behind. Libby walked away from the building, never to return.

Between the first Apocryphon *and the second, there is a shift of personality. What could be considered normal behavior for a child diverges wildly by the second writing, indicating sociopathic tendencies. Although Libby exhibits the escalation of brutality from animal to human subjects, she doesn't seem to repeat these offenses, which is atypical for sociopaths. However, her behavior in detachment and lack of empathy is typical.*[4]

Debate remains as to whether the Apocrypha only mark the first of each phase of Libby's experiments, or if indeed she only conducted one event at each stage. The first two Apocrypha remain nearly emotionless, whereas the third takes on a slightly different tone and it is believed that Apocrypha III and IV may have been written by Libby. Contention exists as to whether she wrote the first two, or if an unknown source fictionalized all of it.[5]

APOCRYPHON III—RESEARCH

She graduated from high school at sixteen and gained her doctorate in entomology by twenty-two. She became a forensic expert in decomposition and the insects that populated the fleshy worlds of the dead. The microscopic realm of insect biology was as interesting as discovering that first maggot-ridden body.

Libby laid her groundwork well, knowing cell structures, the chemical interactions that drove ants, dragonflies, leafhoppers, moths, and the basis of different groups of social insects. Colonies and hives were fascinating in the caste structure of workers and drones. Not all ant colonies had only one queen and most workers were females, sometimes able to breed when necessary. Often drones lived only long enough to fertilize the queen before dying. In some species of wasps and bees the queens mated with multiple drones and stored the sperm, releasing it over time to fertilize the continuous cycle of egg laying at their discretion.

Libby stored the information, then began to study communication of hymenoptera; the bees, wasps, ants and their hives, colonies and social structure. She ordered yellow crazy ants from the Christmas Islands, Western honey bees and Buff-Tailed bumblebees, Asian giant hornets and German wasps. Besides hymenoptera, she brought in Kirby's Dropwing dragonflies from Namibia, Meadow Argus butterflies from Australia, ladybugs from Canada and a host of other species. She concentrated on the pheromone trails of ants and tried to see if she could colonize species that were not hymenoptera. She tried to form messages from light, from chemicals, from Braille-like forms. Diligently, for five years Libby tested many types of command or communication and searched for any effect on hive activity, caste structures or mating.

Her tests did not lead to any discernible change. Her research could have gone on forever. There were always many new paths to take in studying class Insecta. An estimated thirty million species were still unclassified, but Libby grew unsatisfied, feeling that she was not attaining her goal fast enough.

It dawned on her that though she had concentrated on hymenoptera for their social behavior that she herself was not social. How could she possibly understand such behavior unless she undertook the final phase?

First tidying her lab, Libby took two weeks off, leaving as many insects with the department as she took. After all, she worked alone and was known to keep to herself.

She went downtown and entered a department store. For the first time ever, Libby felt a bit displaced, as if she were an ant that had lost all pheromone signals to the colony. Bewildered, she stared at the array of cosmetics, jars and pomades, lotions, scents, eye and lip colors that surrounded her. Turning a slow circle, she could not pinpoint a place to begin until a clerk approached her.

"I want..." She made a motion around her face, struggling for what to say.

The clerk smiled and beckoned her to follow. "I know. You've not worn makeup before. Don't worry, I'll show you what you need. With your features, you don't need much but we can enhance and highlight what you have."

Libby sat through the experience, finding it alien, then proceeded to buy clothes that were more than utilitarian.

Always a good study, she had no problem in applying the makeup. She slipped on a slinky, red spaghetti strap dress that showed her long legs. Red stilettos added to her color and then she made her way to where males swarmed. The lights and music throbbed around her, pulsating off her skin. She danced awkwardly but it seemed to matter little to the men that grabbed her about the waist and pulled her close.

The first man offered to take her somewhere else. Libby freely gave up her virginity in a car. But she did not stay, exiting for the next nightclub. The second man took her in the restroom, and a third in the back alley where they went to "share a joint." At the end of the night, Libby went with five men, finally finding herself in a threadbare hotel room with a naked flickering bulb. She pulled the closest one to her and kissed him, undoing his pants. When he tried to push her head down, she pulled back and sat on the table, pulling up her dress to take him in. It wasn't long before the others followed.

Libby repeated the swarming for a week, collecting as many men's semen as she could. When she felt she had accomplished that task, now holding enough sperm to release thousands of eggs, she shucked off the mating colors and set to work in her home, which bordered a large, state protected park.

She brought out the terrariums with the various insects and arrayed them about her. From bees, flies, dragonflies, beetles, grasshoppers, moths, weevils, wasps and ants, Libby extracted eggs. She required special tools, often a microscope and careful incubation so that the eggs would not wither. Some she took from the hives about her place and others from the insects directly. When she had a good yield, Libby stripped off her clothing. Under a bright light, she made small incisions on her thighs, arms and abdomen, and inserted a different species' eggs into each opening. Although she felt the pain, it was an abstraction from the task at hand and it only aided her concentration. Overshadowing the pain was a flush of excitement, warmth that spread through her in ways sex hadn't.

As she laid each egg beneath her epidermis, she took out a glass case crawling with army ants. Pressing each bleeding wound shut, she applied the ants along the fleshy rim. The ants in turn seized the edges of the cut in their lightning fast jaws and locked on. Libby felt sharp pricks and then cut off the glossy black bodies, leaving the head and mandibles as sutures. She stood with her stitching of ant heads, and opened all containers holding insects.

A few variants of Apocryphon III *indicate that Libby prayed or cried at this point. These have largely been dismissed as additions by unknown sources that wished to humanize her actions. There is no indication in any Apocrypha that she ever showed intense emotion.*

It is argued that Libby was trying to become an insect and found the only way to communicate was to pass on her knowledge through her cells. Still others believe that she had in fact been imbued with the essence of Insecta from birth. [6]

APROCRYPHON IV-A—METAMORPHOSIS

Naked, Libby walked out her door and into the park. In the white heat of the day she stood beneath the trees, her bare feet burrowing into leaf mold. Feeling the slight ripples in the air about her, she spread her arms. It may be that she knew the secret language of insects and called her disciples unto her with the release of a pheromone borne on her words. In a high voice, she trilled.

They came, great black clouds of pixilating Insecta. The air rippled and thrummed with movement. The green bottle flies with their metallic sheen, the beetles with their chitinous clatter, the buzzing drone of bees, wasps and hornets, the flutter of moths and butterflies, the gnats, mosquitoes, the walking sticks and praying mantises. They came from miles around. Still they were only representatives of the greater horde, but one came of every type, thirty million strong.

Onto each pore and hair the smallest insects landed, followed by others, coating her arms, her legs, her naked torso, her face and eyes and ears. When nothing could be seen but the pulsating cluster, it rose into the air, higher and higher, like an enormous runaway swarm. Lifting to the heavens like a gyrating, buzzing black host, it grew smaller and then...dispersed, scattering insects like seed pods.

APOCRYPHON IV-B—METAMORPHOSIS

Libby walked naked amongst the trees under the moon's silvering light. Like Lilith in the Garden of Eden, she moved with confidence. The air seemed to blanket her as she raised her slim, bare arms to the heavens and she cried out in a voice like the chirrup of locusts. Into the skies, boiling from the ground, the myriad host arrived on the pheromone trail, the Insecta in their glory of gold and red, gunmetal black and blue, jarring green and earthy brown, a scintillating mass of color, of forms soft and furred, hard and chitinous. Sound rose like a roar, a thunder, an unearthly humming.

Those who heard the cacophony of wings and legs, and clatter of millions of mandibles thought the end was near. The insects came from all around, swarming up her legs, onto her head. Then they burrowed, chewed and crawled within her. Some crept in her nostrils, others into her eyes, while flies and gnats filled her ears. Other vermin and plump larvae wriggled up her legs. All made their own way and she said, "I am of the hive. Eat of me and understand."

She did not scream nor run, but stood, her form limned in an odd moving pointillism. When an hour had come and gone the insects pulled back as if one and departed. Where they had been, nothing remained; not bone, nor hair, nor flesh, nor sinew. It was as if she had never been.

Her name could have easily been Deborah or Melissa or Mariposa, as would befit a benefactor of insects. Swarmings happen from time to time near urban centers yet no specific incident can be pinpointed in North America where a woman was consumed by insects. There is no extant evidence that she existed under any of these names; that she wasn't a myth generated for a troubled world of the new millennium.

Is this a metaphor in which Libby imparts her knowledge to the insect race, raising them up to the next level of evolution? Indeed, praying mantises have been known to lose wings and then regain them in a single generation—a startling discovery even before the Apocrypha *were created.*

More disturbing is a concept in which few scientists give credence (indeed, they refuse to even look at it), that Libby did indeed pass the mantle of a superior thinking race onto insects, and that homo sapiens' days are numbered. The aforementioned child with compound eyes supports this belief. She not only exhibits the ocular anatomy of Insecta, but displays disturbing digestive traits as well as the ability to communicate and direct insects in hive activities. However, this mutation also supports the argument that due to climatic and environmental changes the human race is evolving into something...else.

There are only four Apocrypha (Discovery, Experimentation, Research, and Metamorphosis), *which coincidentally compare to the four stages of insect growth: egg, larva, pupa and imago. Since the appearance of the first* Apocrypha, *global warming and pollution have seen the extinction of many amphibious species that kept insect populations in check. As well, entomologists have recorded a change in hymenoptera hive and colony organizations and structure, as well as the evolution of some other orders into new, highly organized social structures.*

The question most debated about the Insecta Apocrypha *is who wrote them? If Libby did exist and if she did not write them, then the only living beings that saw her deeds were the insects.* [7]

Footnotes

[1] Alice Rothwell, ed. <u>Sacred Writings of the Modern Cult Movements in North America</u> (New York: Random, 2014)

[2] Rachel Urghart and Roy Hammerschmidt, eds. <u>Exegesis of the Insecta Apocrypha,</u> Rabbi Joel Shapiro, Chapter 1 "Interpretations of the Soul" (Numinous Press, Toronto, 2032) 14

[3] <u>Sacred Writings</u> Shandra Radakrishnan, Chapter 3 "Psychoanalysis of the Messiah and Anti-Messiah in Relation to Major Religions" 39-46

[4] <u>Sacred Writings</u> Radakrishnan, 53-56

[5] <u>Exegesis</u> Carl Purdy, Chapter 5 "Interpretations of Voice" 76-78

[6] <u>Exegesis</u> Purdy, 112-115

[7] <u>Exegesis</u> Shapiro, "Conclusion" 198-220

ON WINGS OF ANGELS

Waking is as hard as sleeping on wings of angels. Not the downy softness we had superstitiously believed. I have to be careful not to roll too suddenly onto sharp-edged pinions; I already wear the badge of small red scratches. Clouds outnumber angels; silver, ivory, shades of billowing gray, and blue. In that roiling stew of wind-stirred cotton I am the flesh. It is the sound that always wakes me, not trumpets or ethereal choirs, but the ominous rumbling of clouds meeting and the sharp snap and rustle of angel wings flexed.

Armageddon, people had cried. God has forsaken us. Only true believers need apply. Why angels chose the skeptic, I'll never know. It was worth it, after admonishing end-of-the-worlders to deal with their lives and stop pinning hopes on fantasies, to see their shocked, reddening faces as *I* was plucked away. Then again, I was just as surprised.

Why, I asked. To see our point of view, they said. So *they* will stop praying to us.

I'm not an angel, I said. My view will always be different.

They looked heavenward and yawned perfect yawns. Rather than fly over God's flock, they prefer to hang in the air, silent, unmoving, as varicolored as the birds. The old painters came closer than modern romantics who would flinch when angels fight, just like birds over a thrown scrap of bread.

I am ready to return. I don't know which one brought me; there are so many. Even with celestial eyesight, angels rarely watch our world. The clouds are everywhere and they would have to fly too close to people's prayers. It is their watching that unnerves me. It is like the vulture waiting for the man to die. Those on Earth would do better not to dream of angels.

PHOENIX SUNSET

Cracker Jax sat on the worn ashen steps of the old gallery, flanked by two slumbering stone lions. He twisted the colored, UV inhibiting field rings in his ear and stared at the few gun embellished Technos and flashy Cybers striding by in the grayish light. Jagged colors in green and orange shot up his skintight pant legs, adding brightness to the insipid day.

He tensed, then resumed twisting field rings, chin in hand.

"Yo, Jax. Unhinge your mind from the grids. I've got a flash."

Cracker Jax glanced up. "Ember." He ignored her and stared into the street. Ember, a sweep of crimson, dropped beside him and watched his profile. Blood red hair shadowed her skin as her fiery lips brushed his ear with a whisper.

"Cracker Jax, my Cyber cynic, how would you like to play with fire?" She ran glinting ruby nails through his close-cropped hair, heat pulsing from her palm implants.

Jax snapped his finger pinpoint lasers to standby, slammed a hand to his chest, flesh rippling and sheathed under the insul shirt, and hissed air through his teeth, honing sonics. He quickly shifted and seized one of Ember's bird-thin hands. "I'm ready, babe. Your tech magic against mine."

Ember's pupilless red eyes widened. "Hey, just a joke. No scam here. I wanted your attention."

He released her hand. "Don't ever threaten me—even as a joke."

She pushed her hair behind delicately pointed ears. "Well, you're in one iced-out mood. Look," she leaned forward intently. "I've got a quest. A rumor to dispel your dark day. A hunt." Her smile uncovered even rows of ivory teeth.

Cracker Jax shut down his armaments, leaned back on his elbows and asked, uninterested, "What hunt? Some Technos gone razing?"

"No." Ember clacked a gemstone nail against her teeth. "A myth—a real one. One of my spells gleamed a phoenix. Nearby. No genufactured, Techno made bird. The real thing."

"Imposs," snorted Jax. "You've been sniffing neuro-sen. There's never been real magic in the world. That was proven."

"Wrong-o, Cynic." Ember fished within her voluminous jacket and pulled out a can of 'brosia. She broke the seal, pulled at the drink and passed it to Jax. "There's always been magic-*that's* been proven, when the reality rifts brought faery and humans face to face. You accepted that magic. It's only magical animals both races have glammed as unreal."

Jax swished the 'brosia over his teeth and swallowed. "So what's the spout on this phoenix then?"

"That's just it." Ember's hands flashed, sparking light back to the ozone grids overhead. "I've divined it and it's near. I want to find it, prove one way or the other... It could be ultima max."

Jax raised his eyebrow. "And you want my aid."

"Come on, Jax. An adventure. You're just brooding bad times. 'Sides, I need your search skills."

He laughed abruptly and threw up his hands. "All right, Ruby Red. Tell me more about this rare chicken."

She stood, pulling Jax's thickly muscled arm. He rose and they walked down the steps, boot heels scraping stone. "No chicken. Legend says only one exists at a time. Shows up just after or before its death. Rebirths itself, you know. Some sort of immortality/sun sym."

Cracker Jax dropped his arm on Ember's narrow shoulders. "That's it? It'll turn out to be some mutant fowl. The giant chicken that ate the world. The chicken shit alone would kill us." He ducked as if something was falling on him but straightened at Ember's scowl.

"What's it look like?"

"Scan your linkup files, grid brain. The info's there under myth. We'll need gear. It's cozed up in the non-grid wastelands."

Jax pressed deep brown fingers to his temples and whispered file commands. He stopped. "You mean we're going into contam land for a wild goose chase for some..." he echoed the inner voice. "...Some 'symbol of rebirth, the phoenix rising from ashes'? That's it?!"

Ember's voice trembled but she continued flippantly. "Open your orbs. If it's real then chance is we might fly free of all this." Her hand swung up to encompass buildings and cracked roads shimmering red under the UV grid's garish light. "It will mean that we can ice those contam lands. It will mean that there is true magic and if that bird can rebirth itself maybe, just maybe its power can help us help..."

Her voice trailed off as her hand trembled and sunk to her side.

Cracker Jax shook his head. "All right, all right. Don't throw your stash away. Come on. I think Tinder has some rad suits."

An hour later they entered a slouching burb house surrounded by cascading mounds of brick and board. They found Tinder crawling under a table, cursing. The dwarf's mohawk was dusty from rooting in piles of fabric and scrap metal. He quickly scrounged up two rad suits and a rickety scooter full of dints.

Ember struggled into the crinkly silver suit. "Are you sure I need this? We aren't usually scathed by contam like you humes."

Tinder picked at an emerald tooth and grunted. "You may not need field rings when in the Fey holms or the city but I wouldn't press my luck in high contam areas. There have, after all, been mutated Fey born."

Jax grinned. "Yeah, it's only right you suffer some if I have to." He pushed a thin metal band, lightly etched with gold lines, around his forehead and twisted the three beads on it. A low hum filled the air as the protective field enclosed him.

Ember snapped on her band then looked askance at the scooter. "How's this thing to work again?"

Chains clattering around his wrist, Tinder dropped three coppery disks into her palm. "Put one of these in the fuselage slot, heat it and recite the spell for flight. It should do the trick."

Ember nodded and tucked the microchip embedded disks into a hip pocket.

Cracker Jax passed Tinder a small sack of noncontam rations and saluted. "Thanks. We're off to hunt legend."

They rolled the scooter past the metal mounds and onto a rendered pavement slab. A disk between her palms, Ember voiced a code command and heat glowed from her hands. Jax gingerly picked up the glowing disk with a gloved hand and pushed it into the slot as Ember intoned the spell. They mounted and the scooter made no sound as it moved beneath them.

They drove past cement and glass Techno towers, through several Cyber burb clusters of wood and concrete constructs and near a Fey stronghold of lush green trees kept alive by magical enhancement.

As they journeyed, the grids thinned until only the somber sky, cloaked in clouds, remained. The stillness thickened and stark trees brandished accusing limbs.

Lightly clasping his waist, Ember spoke into Jax's multi ringed ear. "Should be triflin' to trace. Aren't any animals to gum the infra tracery." Jax nodded, tight-lipped.

They drove through the calm quiet and entered a miasma of roiling sky and land the color of old ash. Old landfill eruptions spotted the earth, metal barrels spread helter skelter. Ember pointed to one jumble. The faded black rad sign, its three triangles, apexes touching, still glowed.

Bleached bones of a massive animal bloomed like a sad flower, reminding them of the initial seed that had grown such a garden. Ember's pale skin lightened until her hair and lips looked like wounds. Cracker Jax frowned, knuckles almost white upon the handlebars.

They stopped by the cadaverous remains of a squat building. Jax touched his metal headband. "Are you sure this is the area, Ember?"

She nodded, hugging herself. "I can taste it, you know. This," her arm moved jerkily, "place. All this contam, I feel it icing the land."

Cracker Jax grabbed a pack from the scooter. He spoke a quick voice command and blinked his eyes in a pattern of long and short winks. "Well, let's find this bird then. Infra's on." He scanned the landscape. "Hmm. I can see the rad hot spots but should still be able to trace any life forms. Which way?"

Ember pointed east, away from the crumbling road. She chattered nervously as they moved out. "I think this is the Ace, Jax. To find life, to find a phoenix, especially in the rad lands would mean there's still magic; a world life force."

Jax, looking, scouting, said nothing. Ember talked on until Jax stopped and scrutinized her face. He lightly touched her shoulder.

"You know, before the reality rifts people thought elves, satyrs, dwarves...thought all of you were just faery tales, myth. There was that romantic idealism to hang onto, a life more magical, better attuned. I think people had more hope when they thought magic might exist." He shook his head.

"Then came the reality rifts. The Fey seemed just as fallible as humans and there was nothing left to believe in."

Ember shivered. "I think the Fey brought their own demise through their arrogance, using magic so freely. If they'd been tuned, then the rifts between techs and faery wouldn't rule." She poked her chest. "That's why I turned Cyber and why this phoenix is the ultima max. There's still hope and a chance that the land might sprout some buds. Agree?"

Jax smiled a lopsided grin. They continued searching.

After combing the area for several hours they moved closer to a turgid soup of water and debris. It rippled sluggishly, popping up lumpy shapes. They halfheartedly poked around in a forest of crackly branches and spires of dead trees. Night dyed the clouds black.

Jax, hands on hips said tersely, "I don't think we're going to find anything. Any of these hotspots could be a bird or just more rad."

Ember sighed, shoulders slumping. "You're right. I don't want to snooze in no man's land. Let's skim."

They walked away from the shore passing a small gully. Cracker Jax glanced back at the lake then caught a flash of color that showed even without the infravision. He grabbed Ember's sleeve. "Wait. Over there."

Like a blazing fire, something pulsed, fluttered amongst the broken tree limbs.

"Goddess, it's so beautiful," Ember whispered as they approached.

Laying before them was an enormous bird, feathers flushed in deep scarlets, vibrant orange, golden yellow. Its three foot tail feathers spread out like rivulets of blood. It flapped a large wing and lay on its side panting.

Jax kneeled down, frowning. "Something's wrong. It's sick."

Ember clasped her hands. "Perhaps it's at the end of its cycle, ready to die and be reborn."

Cracker Jax held a brown finger to his temples and spoke a command. "File—Phoenix."

"Hmm. There's a dispute of when they're reborn but who knows when the first existed. It could be at the end of a cycle."

"It must be." Ember approached the bird. "We have to help it. It's supposed to die in a sweet smelling nest."

Jax stared at her back. "How are we to do that? We don't know if it's the phoenix or not. It could be some Techno genufacturing."

Ember's voice quavered. "It doesn't matter. Nothing deserves to die like this. We'll take it back with us. Tend it. We must."

She moved closer, slowly, as if afraid the bird would take flight. Kneeling she reached out to touch it.

Cracker Jax sighed and said gently. "Ember, look at it. It's half the size of me. We couldn't possibly carry it on the scooter." He looked at the bird. "I don't think we'll have to," he added quietly. "It's dead."

"No." Ember cradled its sinuous neck and head in her arms. Its obsidian eyes grew milky. "No. Where's the flames?" She stroked its blood red chest. "Where's the flames?"

Tears etched her face. Jax turned his watery eyes to the ground and began walking away. He heard Ember stand and then a crackling sound grew behind his back. Looking over his shoulder, blinking he saw Ember light the carcass aflame with her eye lasers. She watched until the flames caught, blending with the feathers. The dried branches beneath the bird disappeared in smoke as the fire expanded in a widening circle.

Ember walked to where Jax waited, holding a solitary three foot feather between slim fingers. Her eyes sparkled with tears. "I had to. It deserved a better death than that—a clean death."

Cracker Jax hugged her to him and they turned their backs on the spreading fire, walking back to the scooter, arms around each other. The flames leapt toward the

evening sky feeding color, like feathers afloat, into the
bleakness.

LOVER'S TRIANGLE

It was so cold I expected the ozone grids that waffled the sky to hiss from the rain. They continued to glow a false green. Their reliability didn't matter much; rad couldn't get through with the weather so shitty. The rain wouldn't matter anyway, once inside Fundamental Glue.

I saw the garish orange even in the deluge, and ran to the door. Wiping water out of my eyes, I palmed the door and entered Fundamental Glue. Warm ecstasy. It was dark inside, and my eyes gradually adjusted to the diffused wraithlights that bobbed above each table. Inside was nearly as garish as the front with long diagonal stripes of green, blue and red that covered the kylar plastiplate walls. Keg had taken no chances and had made Glue impervious to almost all types of razing, except for old-world bombs, which no one was fool enough to use. No one in their right minds, but we had long ago lost that perspective.

I walked into the din and pushed through the crowd, close as maggots, to the bar. The place would soon writhe in gyrations of bliss when Bore Hunter started playing. I searched through the mix of humans and Wireheads for Sharman and Claxon but couldn't see them. Turning back to the bar, I yelled at Keg. "Hey, Keg, 'brosia please. How's biz?"

Keg, lean, angular and with a hooked nose, glowered under bushy eyebrows as he filled glasses with coolants. "Not bad, Agate. You gonna read futures tonight?" He plunked the can in front of me.

I patted my coat's pockets. "I've got the decks. Wasn't planning to but maybe I will for a while."

"Please do." He turned away to the far side of the bar and yelled back, "Quiet spot's at the back."

I squeezed by three Wireheads whose eyes sheened with a silvery metal. Probably housed special optics—unnerving to look at them. I bit back an old curse at such unnatural use of flesh. At least it was their bodies, not mine. I sat at a table scarred with initials and faced the stage.

I rooted into one pocket and felt the reassuring presence of stiletto and wand. The decks lay wrapped in silk in the opposite pocket and I pulled one out. The Romany Wanderer. I shuffled through the Gypsy *patteran*—symbols—and decided to use the Mythic deck instead, with its strong traditional images for the Emperor, the Fool, Death, etc.

I laid a piece of red silk patterned with black sickles and roses upon the table, and began shuffling the cards. Eyes closed, I concentrated, centering myself to the earth, letting the sounds of the Glue drift away. Once inner calmness blanketed me, I opened my eyes, feeling connected to the symbolism of the cards. The portents and messages swirled within me, waiting to be released into sequence. I let out a long breath and sipped the 'brosia.

As I shuffled the cards, a shadow fell across the table and I looked up. The wraithlight obscured the features, but by the white skin color it had to be a Wirehead.

"Do you tell futures?"

I looked up into the shadowed face and answered, "Only if you ask."

"Then I ask." He pulled out the chair and sat. Classically handsome, with a strong brow and deep brown eyes. A Roman nose and a narrow chin were framed by auburn hair that just brushed his shoulders. He looked at me, waiting.

I held out my hand. "I'm Agate."

"Gamaliel." He shook mine and I passed the cards to him. I noticed the carbon steel nails and guessed cybersonics or lasers lay beneath them. He set his drink at the corner of the table and said, "What do I do? I've never had a reading before."

"Never?"

"I thought my future was fairly evident." He smiled. Pointed teeth. White skin. One of the undead. I tried to hide my unease.

"Oh, well...shuffle them, keeping the, uh, question you have in mind. When you feel ready, cut them into three piles on the silk and I'll take over from there."

I shivered slightly with dread, but was still fascinated at this man's nonchalance. From the moment I was old enough to understand, my parents and uncles, aunts and cousins, all the Rom had instilled in me the fear of death and the dead. Because my people feared death so much, we worshipped it—no—gave obeisance to keep the dead away. It had always been so: treat the dead with respect and they won't come back to haunt you. It was all I could do to keep myself from chanting a warding spell before this man.

It was difficult, but I recentered myself as Gamaliel cut the cards into three piles. I picked them up, then turned over one after the other until there were twelve in the sunwheel spread, with a thirteenth card in the middle. I pointed to the middle card, the Emperor; an assured man sitting upon the throne.

"This represents you and shows you are strong, a leader. Um, that is beyond your, uh, natural attributes. You're in control." And I wasn't. Undead so close, I was unnerved and feeling foolish. I took a deep breath and tried to get through the reading.

I had forgotten to ask him what his question was. No matter, the cards would still reveal an answer. The past and present cards showed several swords cards, the Moon, the eight, and three of wands, and the king of coins.

I sipped my 'brosia and said, "Your past shows there was a time of confusion and strife, partly caused by your view of magic. You were shaped by it and dealt with a great hardship. But it shows here," I pointed to the wands, "that you have worked hard and become comfortable. You do not want for anything in the world of material gain, and have attained what you tried for."

I looked up and saw he watched me, not the cards. Looking down, I pointed to the next three cards; the knight of wands, the Fool and the queen of cups. "Your future shows that you search for something more and that it will lead you on the Fool's journey. You must be careful, for you might be so blinded by what you seek that you will fall to someone who is charming, yet potentially harmful. You must remember reason, but don't overanalyze the situation."

He picked up his drink and sipped it, still watching me. He hadn't said a word and I wondered about the undead drinking normal drinks.

I licked my lips and continued. "These last three cards show the outcome of what you seek." The cards were strong; the Lovers, the Lightning Struck Tower and the five of cups. I was surprised that the Death card hadn't figured in a spread for the undead. But then, I knew better, that card hardly ever meant the literal interpretation. "Your search will lead you into a relationship, possibly a partnership. This card signifies that you must make a choice and that there is the possibility of rivalry. The Tower indicates sudden change and a collapse of old structures. I don't think this relationship of the Lovers will last through it, but in the end there will be something left to build on. You will find that choices for the future will have changed, and the old beliefs will have broken down."

Gamaliel leaned back in his chair and smiled. "An apt reading, and an interesting one. I should do this more often. Thank you."

I finished my drink and couldn't help saying, "You're not like the others." I had, of course, "encountered" my fair share of roving undead or gangs in this chaotic world.

He leaned forward, elbows on the table, while I avoided his eyes and wrapped the cards in the silk to put them away. I didn't feel like doing any more readings. Too hyped.

"Do you mean, like other Wireheads, or vampyrs?"

"Vampyrs. They're usually not so public, or so I thought, unless..."

He smiled widely, enjoying my discomfort. "I'm not on the hunt, if that's what you're worried about."

"Oh." But how did I know he told the truth? I fiddled with objects in my pockets and tried to maintain the cool facade.

He stood and I realized he was very tall, over six feet. "If you don't mind I'll buy you a drink. Partial payment for the reading."

I just nodded, hoping I wouldn't make a bigger fool of myself. I watched him walk to the bar, calm, barely parting the crowd.

Gamaliel returned and set the 'brosias down. He took off his long, green lacquer plast coat and tossed it on the back of the chair. Its hard scales clattered and caught the wraithlight hovering above. His muscled arms were bare and he wore an insul T-shirt that said "Go with the flow, it's here to stay."

He moved his chair to the side, so he half-faced me, and so that he could watch Bore Hunter, a band of stocky men and women with strobing gemstones adorning their heads. One guitarist had silver tusks that protruded from her lower lip. A singular beauty.

Gamaliel leaned over and whispered, his breath hot and sultry in my ear, "I promise not to drink you if that's what you're worried about."

"Oh." I tried to laugh. "No...well, yes I was. Sorry, but I don't know many...of your type and well, my people have always had a great fear of the dead returning to haunt us."

"And do you think I'm haunting you?"

"No. But you do have to eat sometime."

After watching the band for several minutes, Gamaliel turned to me just when I thought he hadn't heard.

"Yes, I do have to eat, but I choose carefully and usually those who deserve it."

That didn't ease my nerves. I'd met enough crazed Wireheads who arbitrarily decided what someone deserved.

"How do you decide? And wh—what do I deserve?"

Amusement sparked his eyes. "To be paid, for one." He tossed some creds on the table. "Don't worry, I won't touch you."

"That's what you say." I gulped my drink. "How do I know it's the truth?"

"Well," he leaned close. "You just have to trust me. Besides, I know that Gypsies have charms against the undead. I'd have to wait until you didn't suspect me."

I smiled, feeling that I could trust him. My intuition was rarely wrong. I finally relaxed enough to talk with Gamaliel about the city packs, and the music of Bore Hunter, and the other new band, Acid Reign, that was hitting the scenes.

I realized as we talked that my perceptions, and old legends of the undead had clouded my view to the person beneath the vampyr image. Gamaliel talked warmly. I was fascinated by this friendly vampyr. This man could literally give me the kiss of death and yet he seemed at ease, lighthearted. But then, he could be. It wasn't he that had to worry about having his life stolen.

The evening passed and Gamaliel and I danced, sucked into the desperate ambiance of people trying to forget the world. We were still talking when Keg came over and said, "Time to run, folks. I need my beauty rest." I found myself attracted to this man, this dead...thing. He seemed so alive, and yet, again I found preconceived warnings that my people had given coloring my views.

I pulled on my voluminous, many-pocketed coat and patted it to make sure everything was there. Gamaliel stood and pulled on his shiny coat. "Look, Agate, I'll walk you to your place. Too many packs out lately."

"I live at Stanley's Green. That's almost an hour

from here."

He raised one eyebrow and motioned with his arm toward the door. "I have nothing but time."

It was a tomb outside. The rain had stopped. The only sound was the ever-present hum of the grids overhead. We walked down the quiet crumbling roadway, well away from the cryptlike depths of abandoned buildings. Neither of us talked, our boot heels the only living sound.

Suddenly I whirled, the sense of someone watching too strong to ignore. Behind us, emerging from a doorway, were two Gorgon pack members. Their fibril hair writhed about their shoulders. They smiled carbon steel smiles and razor nails glinted in the streetlight. I looked around as Gamaliel turned to face them.

Quickly, I pulled the stiletto and wand from my coat. I waved the wand through the air in a pattern of pentacles and chanted a warding against the Gorgons' hypno-sonic stares. I thumbed the safety on the laser stiletto. The blade hummed and the edge of white light lit my hand.

Gamaliel calmly fished a leather band from his pocket and tied back his hair. "I suggest you hunt somewhere else."

The female Gorgon, her hair ending in arrow-like points, laughed. "Hey, the man's walking his meat."

The other one moved a step forward. "Don't be greedy. There's plenty to share."

And then they were upon us. It happened as fast as lightning, and I managed one stab at the male before Gamaliel kicked him flat, then slashed through the throat of the woman. He bent over the man whose chest he'd crushed. The Gorgon wheezed and moaned. The smell of charred flesh and metallic blood tainted the air.

Gamaliel turned back to me, his lips drawn back from his fangs. He growled, "Turn away. You won't want to watch."

"But, what—"

"Turn away," he snapped, and I did. But I wanted to

watch, like a moth drawn to the deadly flame. Saliva filled my mouth; I felt like vomiting at the thought of him sucking up the warm lifeblood. There was a part of me that said, *this is taboo*, and another part that said, *you can watch; you're not doing it*. I resisted the urge to look.

I jumped when Gamaliel touched my shoulder. He urged me on, saying nothing.

'Just before we entered the green I turned to Gamaliel and said, "Did you have to—"

"Look, you knew what I was. They would have killed us. How do you suppose I feed?" He was angry, but I was scared.

"I saw you drink 'brosia."

The anger left him and he sighed. "Yes, I can drink and eat regular food but my nutrition must be from blood. Oh." He stopped. "I see. Agate," he touched my face softly. "I swear I will never harm you. I only take from those who would do others harm; the evil ones, the flesh packs. Please, trust me."

"Yes, I do," and realized I meant it.

We stopped in front of the door to my cube. Trying to hide the lingering dread of the Gorgon encounter, I bravely invited him in. He declined, saying, "No, it is late and I would rather that you're totally comfortable with my presence. But I would like to talk to you again, if I may."

We agreed to meet at the quieter Schrödinger's Box the following night. I slept deep, and dreamt of walking through tombs, searching, searching, and always behind me someone wailing, "Come back, come back."

It wasn't until our third time together that Gamaliel revealed the extent of his sense of humor. We were sitting on the steps of the old gallery, talking.

"Oh, I brought something for you that I got last night." He dug through his pockets and pulled something out and dropped it in my lap. A red tongue and an eyeball lay shinily on my coat.

I squeaked and jumped up, realizing at the same moment that they were very obvious rubber toys. Gamaliel laughed so hard he nearly rolled down the steps. I slapped him. "Idiot," and had to laugh too. It dispelled my last visions of contemptuous vampyrs.

"You're a very undignified vampyr, you know that?"

He just smirked. I touched his shoulder. "Gama? Would you show me where you live?"

He tilted his head, thought for a moment, and said, "All right."

We walked along crumbling streets, and Gamaliel clasped my hand. I didn't say anything but looked up at him. He looked straight ahead, his head tilted as if listening. I bit my lip but continued to hold his hand. It was warm, not as warm as a living person's, but not the cold of the crypt that I had been expecting.

"What..."

"Shh." He continued to listen.

I looked at the stunted, gnarled trees that lined these streets. Their leaves were few, warped like heated plastic. There had to be strong magic going down to keep them even this alive. I realized we were in Shaughnessy; large houses sprawled across crisp brown grass. Some homes were of stone and others, weather-stripped wood. The ritz used to live here in the twentieth century and it made sense that any ritz left would still live in the spacious homes.

We walked up the cobblestone steps to a house with a turret. The windows were still intact and the door was reinforced with embellished steel. Gamaliel opened the door and let me enter first. If I was expecting tomblike colors and velvet drapes, I was completely surprised. The place was furnished with soft couches, paintings and very little else. Everything numbed my eyes with bright shades of green and yellow.

"Ugh, it's bright in here."

Gamaliel smiled and bolted the door. "It's too

depressing otherwise. But the whole place isn't done in these colors. Here, I'll show you." He led me up a dark wooden staircase. The second floor was more subdued but not somber; the colors ranged through red, green and brown, like a twentieth century forest in fall.

I shivered, imagining Gamaliel dragging victims into his home and keeping them chained in the basement. There was no evidence, but still I quivered, mortal jelly, at what he may have done here. "Very impressive," I said.

He stared down the hall and said, "I am not very old but I was able to find this place before the collapse destroyed too many homes. Except for fortifying, I've had little to repair." Then he turned suddenly and kissed me, holding my shoulders.

Surprised, I looked at him and he stopped, confused.

He dropped his hands. "I'm sorry, Agate. I thought...I hoped. I'm sorry. I wanted you to like me."

"Wait, Gama, I do." I touched his face and dropped my hand. "I do. Why do you think I've spent this time with you?" Why indeed? The lies we tell ourselves. My heart pounded—fear moved like a moist worm into my throat. I swallowed and said, "I do care, very much." Then I kissed him back. The kiss blossomed, grew to many more and then into gentle caresses. He picked me up and carried me to his bedroom. My body responded to his and I clung to him.

We lay, heated by dozens and dozens of candles in his room, but the heat we gave off dimmed them in comparison. Light glittered back from mirrors and windows like thousands of knowing eyes. Tears of sweat flecked our skin.

Gamaliel's flesh shone like a bank of snow against my brown flank. He licked warmly at my neck, my arms, my breasts. I vibrated from his caresses, expecting at any moment to feel the thin sharp bite of his teeth. It made my passion hotter, stronger, thinking that this might be my last act. And I wanted it, I didn't care, to be pulled down and taken at the height of intimacy. What more could I want, taken body and soul?

It was a feeling, not a conscious thought, and it wasn't until years later that I understood what I had wanted.

Later, much later, we lay curled into one another. Gamaliel murmured into my hair. "It is the worst part of this sort of life; the loneliness. So many people fear to be near me and can never relax. There are so many old-world legends, and everyone has preconceived ideas that mold all their views. And my own kind," he laughed bitterly. "They are the worst; egotistical, competitive, jealous. They're happy to perpetrate the image of fear; they love the power, but I don't. I want to love a person."

I turned and looked at him. "Oh, Gama, I don't fear you." I feared myself, my lack of control, and his temptation.

We continued to see each other. Something was happening to me inside that I didn't like; a distorted pearl growing bigger, malignant. Something weighed me down, fought me, changed me. I brooded and provoked fights with Gamaliel, daring him to strike me, to lash out and drain my life. But he wouldn't. He looked at me, hurt.

"Why are you doing this, Agate? Why do you want to fight?"

I snarled, "Do you think it just takes one to fight?"

"No," he said calmly. "No, I don't." And he had turned away.

One night at his place we made love and I finally lay subdued beside him. My mind still roiled and I had grown temperamental over the weeks, afraid of what I wanted and didn't want. The big problem; I didn't know what I wanted, nor why I was angry.

I lay thinking of Gamaliel's long life and my relatively short one. I was more than a universe away from him. He murmured something, kissed my eyes, my mouth and nipped lightly at the flesh of my neck.

I gasped and returned to myself. Trembling, I felt a

yearning to bare my neck—abandon soul and flesh to his caresses. In that moment, quicker than light, I murmured a Rom incantation against vampyrs. He yelped as light arced from my skin to his. An acrid smell filled my nostrils.

Pulling back, Gamaliel hissed, fangs flashing deadly. "How dare you! Have you no trust?" he bellowed. He turned and slashed the stuffed chair beside the bed and kicked it across the floor. It crashed into the wall and glass tinkled from the broken window.

I sat up trembling, afraid that I would die now.

Anguish cracked his voice. "I love you, I would never, never drain your blood! Don't you know that by now?"

Shaken, I knelt where I was, knocking a candle over as I reached for him in haste. "I know, I'm sorry. I w— wasn't thinking. Gama." I tried to reach beneath the red-rimming of his eyes. "I'm sorry. I was scared of my own reactions. I wanted to die. I—I wanted you to take me."

I heard him mumble something about mortals and I flashed resentment. He reached, hesitated, then grabbed my arm. I had eliminated the warding.

"Agate, I could make you vampyr. I can give you the kiss of eternal life. Won't you take it; be eternal with me? You need never fear again and we could be together."

"No, I can't, I can't." I shook my head, trying to escape the black pit that threatened to swallow and mold me into something dark, too powerful. "I—my people, we had strong taboos against the undead. Now I know why. I'm sorry. I'm too afraid. I don't think I would be like you, so noble. There is so much power. The Rom knew this, knew it could get out of hand and I never understood it, until now. I don't think I want eternal life."

"Why? Isn't it just a lesser of two evils? We would be eternally together. And there are ways to kill us. You can end it when you want."

I clasped my arms, cold in spite of the candle flames. I wanted it so badly. To live forever, to wield such power. I shook my head, crying, "I—I can't, Gama." I realized then, right to my frozen marrow, that I could never love him properly, for there was another to love.

There were tears in his eyes. He sensed that it was more than his offer that I denied. "Don't you see?" I whispered. "It is death I court, that I am infatuated with. I've used you to get close to death. To be kissed by you, to be loved by you was like loving death—embracing it. I'm so sorry—so sorry." I hugged him tightly now. "I do care for you, Gama, but every time I'd be with you I would see my death and be tempted by it. But the power, the power is too much."

"No!" He tore himself away from me and fled into the night. I didn't wait for his return. I dressed and left. I had gone for the darker lover while Gamaliel had tried to lead the life of the living, not the undead.

We remained friends, albeit distantly. I could not stand to be around Gamaliel and see the hurt in his eyes. *Respect the dead and they won't come back to haunt you.* He walked as if wounded, and I knew I had dealt the most deadly blow to a dead man trying to live.

ICE QUEEN

n the fjords there is a song they sing about ice. There are no two words to describe ice, nor ten, nor a hundred, nor thousands. There is only one word that embodies ice's true meaning. Each person learns to fear ice, and to respect and honor it. By the time a child is old enough to walk it understands the nature of ice. If not, the child dies. Ice has many guises. One spends a lifetime fighting or controlling it, and its one true name is death. It is worshipped, not because it is death, but because it brings life. For ice, at times, must break and melt.

Janie Blue contemplated her relationship with ice as she suited up. Feelie suit snugged her skin, touching her neck, thighs, inner knee, close fit into crotch, under breasts, in armpits. She squirmed at the intimacy, getting ready for a machine to do more than mindfuck her. Complete invasion, complete immersion. All in the name of science; all in the name of work. Icebreaking was the dream and the reality.

Going into a netwalker's nightmare, trying to thaw the ice that had frozen the systems. Janie Blue—the Ice Queen, yet she never got used to icebreaking, no matter how many times she did it. But the pay was good, and hell, the journeys were addictive, if deadly. Landscapes beyond dreams, to control and make her own.

"Icebreaker, are we ready to go?" blared the tinny voice through the barren room.

"Yeah, yeah, gimme a minute to bond, all right." She scratched under the collar and donned the thin, crinkly silver gloves. Picking up the helmet and mouthjack, Janie Blue walked to the cage and mounted the steps. She felt both naked and clothed, the suit so comfortably conforming to her body that she could forget it was on.

"Icebreaker, better hook up the IVs."

She paused, then pulled on the thin metallic socks. "I'm not going to be gone that long."

There was silence on the other end and then, *"You may be. We lost one early yesterday to this glitch."*

"Lost one?" her voice rasped out harsh, demanding. "I should have been told this the moment I was called for the job. What happened?"

"Cabbage."

Shit. For a moment she thought of walking; once you cabbaged there wasn't much mind left to come back to. But her curiosity, which dragged her into the business in the first place, won out. "Was the icebreaker experienced?" There was always the chance that a green icebreaker might have tripped the security programs before doing repairs on the system.

"Two years."

Not that experienced then. Could have been a mistake and not a killer job. Best way to join the cabbage patch though, was to make assumptions. She'd done well by not assuming and not trusting on face value.

"Convince me why I should do this job? And if I do, I want danger pay."

"How much do you want?"

Janie Blue named an exorbitantly high price, angry that Control hadn't given her the specs ahead of time, and after a pause, Control granted it. Surprised, she didn't show it to the cams. When Control didn't balk, it meant it was bad, very bad.

"I also want full stats on this project while I'm going in. Everything, from initiation and purpose of the project, to when and how things started to ice—and what happened to both the netwalker and the icebreaker. And let's also find out why there's such a rush on this." She turned on IV and the evac unit, feeling the little pricks into her skin, then closed the door of the round, hard, fibrous plastic cage. She stood with arms crossed, not yet connecting the electrodes. "I'm waiting."

"Stats are as follows: Genutronics is the third largest genetic and electronic research facility in the world. Specializes in adapting people for specific tasks and habitats using cybernetic enhancements. Some are computer enhanced, but there's not much info. Their main goal for the future is to be able to man space stations, underwater projects and inhospitable planets for long periods of time.

"Have they been successful?"

"Usual success within genetic manipulation parameters. You know, new strains of seeds, better breeds of cattle, that sort of thing. So far, no report of successful human genetic engineering beyond basic embryo development."

"How's electronics fit into that?"

"They are developing systems for maintaining and evaluating physiologies, and are leaders in medical research equipment."

"And why the rush?"

"Uhh, good question. Time sensitive virus could be unleashed, is all they'll say."

Two networkers injured, yet Janie Blue was one of the best. "Okay fine, I'm going in but I have a few more questions. Make sure the neuro-stim is hooked up in case."

"You got it, icebreaker. Ready?"

"Hit it."

A low mechanical purr started up and the ball with human hamster, Janie Blue, rose and bobbed between strong magnetic forces. Janie Blue closed her eyes, settling the helmet on her head and adjusting the jack's mouthpiece. Then she opened her eyes to the cool blue of the system void.

The activated implant behind her ear whispered in a bee voice. *"Okay, here we go, one roller coaster ride coming up."*

From the words, not the neutral, mechanized tone, Janie Blue thought it was Rodrigo guiding her along. She was grateful to have an experienced controller.

Janie Blue saw the flat blue lightening to a pale gray,

and flashes of light began to speed by. Dimension began to form. The lights slowed, and familiar grid patterns of the computer system began to align. All computerized equipment used a similar format, although structures and shapes within the grids varied greatly. She moved her limbs, refamiliarizing with the appearance she now took. Here was where the human Janie Blue was left behind and the icebreaker took over. Like every icebreaker, Janie Blue, with the controller's help, could activate the small nurse chip in any system that was set up for human intervention. Each icebreaker carried a corresponding doctor chip. She preferred to call the chip a polyp.

Only icebreakers could get past the simple range of VR feelie suits, and actually reformat the chips into any electronic tool needed while thawing the ice in a down system. It had become a type of mind manipulation over matter and as yet no one quite knew why only certain people could bond with the chips.

"Okay, Control, I'm in. Are the tool programs primed and ready to go?"

"*Sure thing, icebreaker. Vector south southeast by seven degrees and you'll come upon them.*"

"Okay. Tell me what iced the system and what happened to the netwalker and the icebreaker." Janie Blue moved forward, walking naked, for although networkers wore the suit in real-time, everyone first imaged into a system naked. She enjoyed the rush that flushed her body, anticipation of the adventure, unknown dangers. *Going to pit flesh against machine. Easier than dealing with people, any day.*

No one had yet been successful in getting anyone to feel like a machine while using the feelie wear. Humans could only imitate and feel like living creatures, just as all computer and system programs could only imitate nonliving things completely. From time to time Janie Blue had come across jungles, deserts or even animals imaged by security systems, however there was always a two-dimensional appearance to a system-run construct. So she walked to where the security codes, fixit and doctor programs waited to be wielded in fixing Genutronics' system.

Control continued, *"Netwalker was doing what netwalkers do—her weekly system maintenance check, viewing programs for bugs. Found her* In Specs *were losing light and definition. Began her usual save and exit, tapping the pad, when the system flared into her* In Specs *and blinded her. Looks like she'll keep her vision in one eye but has lost partial in the other—"*

"That shouldn't have happened. There are safety controls in almost all but the most archaic *In Spec* systems. Even then, they're not equipped to be dangerous."

"You telling me. Specs *checked out as being in prime shape but the chip was reconfigured. Next, icebreaker went in. He reported A-Okay until he entered one structure that seemed norm for security. Believe he said it was a pyramid. Next we knew, cabbaged."*

"Great. What security system does Genutronics use?"

"Won't say. Classified. The basic is AJar but all we know for the red code is that it's top line, developed by their think tank specialists."

"Great," she muttered quietly. "Time sensitive virus, classified security, cabbaged and blinded people. Just great." Janie Blue reached the cache, which, as part of the security invasion program, included a suit that was really a camouflage security code so she could code walk through safety perimeters. As she dressed she checked the doctor programs and found them top-line. If any of these instruments of technical healing didn't do the job, then nothing but total system shutdown and purge would. A belt held the smaller serviceable tools and the inoculation guns.

She surveyed her surroundings. Fairly standard neon green grids all around, icicles hanging from them. Nothing differentiated one direction from another, or where the main program resided. It really fooled no one. All grids ran to the mainframe sooner or later.

"Shortest route please."

"East southeast and full speed ahead."

Janie Blue smiled. "Thanks, Rodrigo, I'm proceeding."

"Aw, you recognized me. Good luck, Ice Queen."

"Thanks, keep me tuned to my stats."

She concentrated, activating the chip and the camo suit's circuitry, and imaged the shape of an albatross. She flapped powerful wings, and sped over the grids, towing tools and guns. Something formed on her horizon line. As she neared, she made out the bright pixel-lighted shape of a pyramid, Aztec style. The other icebreaker had been cabbaged by entering it. Perhaps he had been unstable before the job. She laughed mirthlessly. As if they all weren't a bit unstable; they snapped up chances to spend reality in the unreal. And Janie Blue, like all icebreakers, seemed to mesh better with machines than people. Machines were predictable. They didn't have erratic emotions.

She decided she would climb the pyramid, though she could have easily flown over it, but that might not get her through the first line of defense.

She set down, wings and taloned feet retracting back into a now human body clothed in feathers and animal skins, paint striping her arms and gold adorning her ears, nose and neck. Aztec dress for an Aztec front. Mounting the steps, Janie Blue looked at the security construct and marveled at the sophistication in the background details. Petroglyphs and carvings covered the painted stone. Momentarily disoriented from the image's reality, she had to remember that it was still a construct, but better than most. Parrots in emerald and azure flew overhead, calling out and rustling the trees that now crowded the horizon.

She reached the top and there, lying on the center stone, was a woman. No—it vanished, then the image reappeared, the face smiling up at her. When she looked closely she realized that it was a machine, a robot with tiny rivets and shiny flesh-colored metal. Like one of those pin-ups from the 40s. The eyes glowed eerily and the robot said, "You know what you have to do."

Janie Blue narrowed her eyes and warily watched the machine. Was it a trap to snare her? This had to be a security system barrier. Her tools contained some of the passwords to break through to the main systems so she could find the glitch. Therefore, this must be part of the glitch. She chewed her lip.

The system was very intricately designed if it could play on human aversion for taking another life. It was obviously a test.

"My pleasure," smiled Janie Blue, and took a security-encrypted blade from her belt and plunged it into the woman-robot's heart.

The imitation flickered and disappeared, a voice laughing, "I'll see you soon."

"You're through first level security, Janie Blue. Be careful. Heart rate's up but still within normal parameters."

She wasn't worried. AJar was tough even with the codes, but she had broken into enough AJar systems before. Formulating a condor, Janie Blue grew wings and flew from the pyramid, which dwindled to nothing as soon as she left it. Landing now on a grid made up of flat triangles, she looked about. A platform and table appeared. Cautiously, she walked over and noticed something that looked like a wrench on a chair. The wrench grew, expanded and rapidly unfolded like a map into a robot with a monitor for its head, which projected a human face. Janie Blue backed up slowly.

"Welcome, welcome to the friendliest game in town," gestured the robot. "Come on up and play a little hand of poker."

There was something, perhaps the too friendly tone of voice, which warned Janie Blue that this could be the central program glitch. But something was very wrong. Usually the glitches were deeper within, past the security systems that acted like white blood cells, not realizing they were protecting the infection from the cure. It almost seemed as if this glitch was running the security. And it was too easy. It should take much longer just to get through the security systems to be able to work on the iced program.

She hated the imagery, yet was drawn to it. There was a twisting of thoughts and time that icebreakers adapted to, but when they exited the mainframes the addiction for the colors, the images and the interaction so unlike everyday life snared them with a hunger to return again and again to this unreal reality. Janie Blue especially liked the lack of close interaction.

She had always thought to control what she did, but she knew, after years of breaking ice, that the machine controlled her. She could only retaliate by going back in and manipulating the systems for that fleeting image of order within her life, that strange dangerous peace that she craved. After all, she had never had luck in commanding her emotions or others' actions. Here was the only control.

"Rodrigo, where in the program am I, can you tell?"

There was too long a pause. *"Weird. You just break through several security codes?"*

"Only one."

"You're on level five security. Genutronics says there are five levels to their AJar, and another three to the other system. You've somehow been bumped along, which must mean even the security systems are glitched."

"Yeah," Janie Blue pondered and stared at the table with its robot dealer. "I'm picking up some strange imagery. I hope you've given me the best doctor programs available, and the security codes."

"You bet. Get to the right spot and the fixit will do the trick. As to the security codes, Genutronics supplied them encrypted, reassembled at your end. They should work."

She grunted. Weird was right. Icebreakers were sworn to secrecy on projects, and as neutral as judges. Doctors of the net. The drug and the drugged. Few, if any, had ever broken icebreaker ethics. After all, few icebreakers cared enough for human politics to ever get involved, and Janie Blue was no exception. Yet Genutronics wouldn't reveal their security codes, which would be changed after an icedown anyway. They weren't telling the whole story.

She constructed a shimmering aura bubble, then walked up to the table, eyeing the robot B-movie-style construction. Its spindly neck swiveled, the monitor watching her, exclaiming, "Yesiree, folks, come right up and try your hand at the game of poker. More skill than chance, so take a chance and play."

She sat and the table began to spin, or rather the surroundings spun and Janie Blue had to focus on the table to fight down the vertigo. "I'll play but we use my cards." She grabbed the level five security code off her belt. She put it on the table and it was a deck of cards.

"You're invading," said the robot, its image flickering and changing as it dealt the cards.

"I'm not." Janie Blue picked up her cards. "I have permission to be here." She looked up and jumped.

"But it's my body," said the now almost human-looking man sitting across from her. His eyes glowed digital orange and his fingers were metal. Yet, he was the best human construct she had ever seen.

"We're playing five-card stud, cross-eyed jacks and drunken deuces are wild." He smiled and looked at his cards.

She looked down, thinking furiously, and noticed the deuces did indeed reel about on the card. She had no cross-eyed jacks, but two dancing eights, a sleeping king and a four that looked to be shaking little fists at her. How could the system be manipulating the security code configurations? Sorting her cards, she said, "Your body is in service to Genutronics. Your purpose is in storing, evaluating and tabulating information."

The four spit electric sparks that flew at her face and deflected off her shield. She flinched but discarded the four, received another card and placed it in her hand. It was another eight. She looked up, her eyes hurting from the moving images. The robot had taken three cards and looked at her. "Indeed? And what does your body do? Call."

What did it mean? Was it saying that her body stored

information too and therefore belonged to Genutronics?
"No money?"

"No money, no chips. The stakes are higher."

She laid her cards on the table, "Four of a kind, eight high."

Still smiling, he—it looked at her and laid his cards out. "Three of a kind, ace high. You win this round." Everything winked out. Janie Blue fell to the ground, once more in the grid.

"Shit! Which way, Rodrigo?" She stood, automatically brushing at her legs before realizing the futility of the motion. There was no dirt.

Again there was a pause before Rodrigo came on. *"Uh, same as before, icebreaker. You're on level one, top security. Three levels in all."*

Janie Blue frowned. Rodrigo usually gave the specific directions again so that there could be no mistakes. She walked on and immediately the ground reformed around her feet into bumpy terrain, fissures smoking and emitting foul-smelling steam. Something large and brown flapped down screeching and clawing towards her. She pulled a security-coded gun and shot. The creature veered off but did not die. She reconstructed her outfit to a thicker, resilient higher security config.

Janie Blue then felt something constricting her legs and waist, crushing painfully into the skin. She looked down and all the security devices had turned into snakes. Shivering, she tore at them and yelled into the mouthjack. "Rodrigo, what the hell's going on? My security codes have gone down as organic constructs. Where's my security passes?" She threw the snakes from her.

"I'm sorry, those were the only ones available. Your heart rate's accelerated, respiration erratic, small contusions to your upper right thigh."

What? Contusions. That couldn't happen! "Get me out of here then. We're going to need a real-time analysis of the system."

"I'm sorry, you must stay and finish the job."
"You're not Rodrigo. What's going on?"
"Please complete the job. Rodrigo has taken ill."

She didn't know who was at the controls now but no controller had ever violated the integrity of an icebreaker's trust before. She'd make sure they'd pay for this—if she got out alive and in one piece. Genutronics wanted answers and would keep sending in icebreakers until one cracked the ice. The only way to survive this glitch meant keeping her polyp, which she embodied, in one piece. Extraction without the proper withdrawal procedures could permanently damage her brain. Her life mattered to her more than Genutronics' games.

Knowing that she was completely alone and unable to trust the person at the controls, Janie Blue made a strong effort to remember her real body in the feelie suit, and reached up to turn off the mouthjack. The effort exhausted her and left her head spinning. Now the only communication would be the stats on her body that Control received until they decided to extract her from the system. If they decided.

She heard the tiny insect-like voices of her implant exclaiming but she tuned them out.

As soon as her hand lowered, the world changed about her once more and became a tree-lined avenue in an idyllic looking land. Was it the next level of security or the computer-run glitch? She walked cautiously down the avenue, carefully watching her setting while inventorying her working tools.

This was unlike any other icedown she had worked on. Security had gone haywire, graphic constructs were much more sophisticated than any she had ever seen, and the system was imaging organic creatures that looked real enough to hurt. It took no dummy to figure out that whatever electronics research Genutronics was involved in had actually invaded their system, or otherwise got out of control. If Janie Blue finished the job, she would levy charges against Genutronics.

She neared the end of the avenue that opened out into pink and green marbled arches and columns. Vines with purple and orange flowers twined about them and birds fluttered by overhead. She looked around, not sure where the next threat would come from. Ahead of her was a Grecian style temple. She mounted the steps and found, sitting just inside the doorway, a man with golden curls, wrapped in a toga, with a strongly muscled chest, sturdy bare legs, and bands of gold about his arms and brow. He stared down at her and her clothes changed to Greek chiton to fit the setting. She stopped, realizing he controlled all of her tools.

"Here, I am god. You must obey my commands or I will kill you."

Janie Blue replied, "A god does not exist without worshippers. Kill me and you have no chance of worship. I think you are a lesser god and must obey the wish of the god Genutronics."

Janie Blue watched him carefully. He could be the unknown security program, or another icebreaker. How else did he manage to look so completely human? Genutronics was playing at something.

His face contorted in anger. "Why are you doing this? You don't have to be here! You're hurting me."

"Possibly, but you have ruined a program according to my information. Not to mention the netwalker you blinded and the icebreaker you sent to the cabbage patch."

"Cabbage patch?"

"He's a vegetable. His mind is gone."

The man before her collapsed, and put his hands over his face. "My mind is all I have." The imagery wavered, like heat waves rippling through air. Suddenly everything was back to the green gridwork of the system with no VR masking. Janie Blue remained in the original suit she had donned. She eyed the construct, trying to figure him out. He still resembled a man but also something more. Had Genutronics really done it? Goosebumps arose along her flesh.

She looked at the man-thing, his upper torso looking human and haggard, but where legs should be there were wheels, gears, metal and plastic. She shivered and hugged herself. "What are you?"

"Lost, lost," he sobbed."

"Do you have a name?"

"I can't remember, I can't remember," he moaned and pulled his hands through now red, now blue hair. It settled into blue and red streaks. "It was Simulat—Simu— Sim...."

He seemed so alone, and Janie Blue almost reached out to him, something she'd never done with a human before. She had to remember that no matter how he looked, he was still just a program. "How about Simon? Would that do until you can remember your name?" He nodded. She introduced herself. "I'm Janie Blue." She continued before Simon lost his vulnerability. "Why did you hurt those who have used the system?"

"They promised me a body but one never came and then one did but I couldn't reach it. Like you, you're occupied. And it hurt, what the other did. They treated me like a highway, as if I were nothing but a—but a machine."

Janie Blue shivered. Occupied. Sure, with electronic impulses that made up her thoughts and personality. "But aren't you a machine?"

He just sobbed in response.

She wished she still had Rodrigo, but he had been removed. That meant Genutronics knew something was different and was treating it as what? Another experiment? With Janie Blue as one of the guinea pigs? And was she being treated like a machine? She realized that she had always been striving to be one. And when the machine seemed to have more emotions than the icebreaker, what did that leave? What was reality, Janie Blue's reality?

She bit her lip and walked a little closer to the man-machine. It was one thing feeling violated doing your job, but it was another thing all together to do someone else's violating. She asked gently, "But aren't you a machine? I mean, we're in a sophisticated program. What are you doing here? If you were machine, you would not have these feelings, and if you were a man, you would not be here." Her reasoning sounded weird but seemed sound.

"Not true, not true," he sighed and looked up at her, wiping his eyes against his arm. "I have felt it every time someone ran their fingers over a keyboard, touching me. And those people poking and probing. It was too much. I couldn't take it. And then...they said it would end with a body," he shuddered. "And then that person invaded me, just like you did, but you played my game at least. You followed the rules."

She felt ill. Hadn't she known someone this had happened to? Someone flesh. Hadn't she felt like this once? Had she been touched this way until she retreated into the machines, escaping the world and her memories, escaping intimacies? Janie Blue swore, uneasy with where her thoughts led her. Simon sniffled and stared at her.

"But why," she knelt beside him and he flinched. "But why are you here? Why are you in the system?"

He shrugged. "Why are *you* here? Why were you born? Do you know, really know? All I know is that I was put here for a purpose, but I've lost sight of that. They grew me but they never said how."

Janie Blue looked at the grid. There were no illusions, no false realities now. Why indeed, was she here? To do other people's dirty work? She had lost sight of her own purpose, and wondered what she really contributed to the world, to herself. She rubbed her forehead and muttered, "I don't need this." To Simon she said, "Genutronics is hiding something. You might be flesh hooked to the computer." Was he the first artificial intelligence, but made of flesh and captured in a machine? If an icebreaker could project thought to manipulate a chip, then it might be possible to meld brains and intelligence with a computer program.

He looked at her, eyes wide. "I can't go on like this, with no contact, never talking to anyone but my own constructs, visits so brief I don't even have time to talk. I want to see the world. I want out of this cage."

Janie Blue wondered how either of them would get out. She stood and paced. "Genutronics wants me to find the ice and break it. That's you. You're icing the system but you're either the system or the program. They're willing to keep me here until the problem is solved or you cabbage patch me."

"Could we fool them?" He stood and watched her pace. "I would rather die than go on like this. But…I don't know, am I flesh outside of here?"

Looking at him, lost and frightened, Janie Blue realized what she needed she would have to find within herself.

Simon watched her warily. Softly, he said, "I just want to be able to decide for myself what I'm doing, what I'm going to be."

She took a big breath. What she was about to propose, she was not sure she could do. She'd always avoided all human contact. "There may be a way, but there's no guarantee that you have a flesh body or that we could even find it when we get out."

Simon's hand grasped her shoulder and it felt real and warm. Her heart banged on her chest.

"I'm willing to take the risk. It's better than this…place."

Janie Blue closed her eyes, and clenched her fists. "Then—you'll need to be part of me, when I leave," she blurted.

"What?" His hand never her left her shoulder. "How? Will I be awake, sleeping? Dead?"

"I don't know. It's the only way." She pulled away and kneeled down. She rushed the words but was afraid if she stopped she'd never finish. "I have a doctor chip embedded in my real-time body and there is one here in the system. It helps me design tools for breaking codes when I'm here. You've been using it to crash the doctor and security programs. At least I think you have. If you can access that chip in my real-time body, you can imbed your "self" in my chip and I can take you out of here. You'll only be a personality, but," she laughed, "that's really all that any of us are, isn't it? Personality housed in some body, whether metal or flesh. I'm not sure it will work, but it's the only way to get by Genutronics' guard. I can tell them I broke the ice. Once out, I can then see about getting you out of the chip. It could take a while to find something…appropriate."

Control's buzzing in her ear told Janie Blue her heart rate was up. She was sweating with dread—anticipation; she didn't know. Then she felt Simon's hand on her chin and she looked up.

He smiled sadly at her and helped her to her feet. "I don't know if I can do that. I'll try. It's scary though. What if I never wake? This could be my last moment alive. And my memories are all I have." He looked down, still for a moment. "I don't remember a mother or father, but I have vague memories of people. I'd like a chance to know who they were."

"I never—I haven't…" She tried again. "I—had—it wasn't pleasant."

Simon's head of tussled red and blue streaked hair tilted and he looked at her quizzically. "You may have as much to lose as me. You don't know what will happen to your mind with me there, do you?"

She tried to smile but couldn't. Shaking her head, she managed to say, "I…never. It's a very intimate thing to share your…mind, your…soul, I guess, with someone. It's scary for me too."

He kissed her then, brushing her lips gently with his. She closed her eyes and allowed the kiss to warm her, and lessen the tension. Then he pulled back.

She opened her eyes to say something to Simon, but he was gone, as was any construct. Only the green lines of the grid showed about her. Green water dripped off of them as if ice had melted there. "Simon?" There was only silence.

Janie Blue made an effort to get the real-time mouthjack back in place. Exhausted, she said, "Control, you'll see the ice is broken. Get me out of here."

"What happened with communications?"

"It interfered with the security reconstruction of the program."

There was a pause, as they checked the system, she presumed. *All right, icebreaker, we're beginning extraction, now.*

As the grid blurred and shifted around her, Janie Blue the Ice Queen had learned something new. An icebreaker didn't always have to break ice, or be ice.

As she opened her eyes, suspended in the cage once more, she had a strong urge to get as far from icebreaking as she could for a while. A drink first, and then some research into Genutronics. She unstrapped herself and as she pulled off the helmet, heard faintly, whispered in her head, *"Janie Blue."*

Janie Blue smiled as she stepped from the cage. Maybe she'd visit the cabbage patch.

In the fjords there is a song they sing of ice. Ice is worshipped, not because it is death, but because it brings life. For ice, at times, can break and melt.

HOLD BACK THE NIGHT

Fireworks went off constantly like machinegun blasts. Chandi opened the blinds and stared out. Through the window, bright lights—white, red, green, blue— littered the sky like a battlefield. Diwali: the festival of lights—to stave back the darkness of the turning year, to hold back Kali's dark embrace.

Kali, the Black Mother of time. Kali the destroyer. It was in Kali's service that Chandi still lived. A devoted follower those many years gone, a priestess.

Chandi sighed and let the curtains drop. She felt uneasy being back in India. There were far too many memories. But the film festival in Bombay, and boredom, had propelled her from New York. As a film critic she had a good reason for coming.

Frowning, she swirled her scotch and drank the last, then donned her wrap and left her apartment. She should have known that being in her homeland would trigger thoughts of her origins.

Born in Calcutta—Kali Cutt to the locals—Chandi had been dedicated at a young age into the sect of Kali. She had held the goats, washed them down, and garlanded them for the sacrifices. As she grew older, she said the sacred rites, anointed the goats, and took the blood to the great statue of the Black Mother. Eventually, she drank the blood in Kali's stead, she slit the throats of murderers and thieves. She had given her life to Kali. In turn, she was given a long, long life to serve Kali faithfully.

She had not been Chandi then, only Kirwa. A lowly, ugly name: Worm. Given to her in hopes that demons would pass her by. In fact, they had not.

She had been taken in Kali's service and deeper into a sect so secret few knew of its dark sacrifices. The demons had made her their own, and, though she changed her name later, it was a worm they had made her. Never again to see the sun; instead, to travel in subterranean blackness and be the lowest form of life. To never know true warmth again.

There had been little reason at first to love or be loved. Carry out the rites of Kali. Carry on as priestess as she had done for decades. And she had been content with that, believing that the rites were all that mattered. Though Kali lived on, the world around her priestesses changed. Times changed, and Chandi changed her name from Kirwa. A lethargy and boredom set in so that eventually she left her homelands to travel far. But no matter how much distance she put between herself and India, she knew she was still Kali's servant. Chandi Kalidas—fierce slave of Kali.

She had loved twice in all those centuries, but the lovers died too soon, giving her a loneliness that gaped like the abyss. She wished she had had the courage to take her life, to end the torturous long days. But the worm of time continued to carry her on its back.

Chandi had been many things through the years, dancing a masquerade that never ended.

She met up with an old friend, and they went to see a movie, a musical. As the swelling soundtrack filled their ears they left the theatre, discussing the film's barely hidden attempts to extol the caste system. In the bright lights and press of so many people, Chandi didn't see the petite woman until she had nearly knocked her over and had to reach out a hand to steady her.

Papers cascaded in chaotic abandon; a couple of books toppled. Chandi heard a muffled "Oh." Then, where she would have expected a curse or a sharp word, the woman turned instead and said, "Are you alright?"

"Yes, but I'm the one who should be asking you if you're alright. I'm very sorry. Let me help."

The woman, who didn't even come to her shoulder, looked in Chandi's eyes, then stopped as still as the warm winter air. Chandi was not surprised. Most people did stare, and in the long years of her life she had seen few of any race with eyes like hers.

"Like a tiger," the woman breathed. "Your eyes are beautiful—tawny gold." Then she caught herself, smiled briefly, and apologized. "Oh, I'm sorry. Really. I didn't mean..."

"It's all right." Chandi laughed, a bit surprised at the woman's candor and reaction. She had grown accustomed to the looks askance, the steps backwards, even in the most modern cities. She gathered some of the fallen papers and handed them to the woman. "I'm used to it."

Her friend called to her, "Chandi, I must leave. Call me tomorrow, alright?"

She nodded absently as she helped the woman. Chandi noticed the petite woman's wavy hair, cut to shoulder length. A pixie chin and classic dark brown eyes, but they were larger, more liquid, with green flecks around the pupil. Peace seemed to flow from her and envelop Chandi.

"I'm Chandi Kalidas."

"Padma Rhaduri. Really, you don't need to help. I can gather these up myself."

"Nonsense. I didn't look where I was going. It's the least I can do." In the humid air, a few papers hung limply from Chandi's hand as she handed them to Padma. [The Survival of Matrilineal Society in Modern India] read one sheet. "This looks interesting. Are you filming this?"

And the conversation had grown wings of its own, had flowed into drinks and a kinship that stunned Chandi in its unexpectedness. Padma was looking for funding for her documentary film. An anthropologist interested in matrilineal societies, she had begun her research as an escape from a bad marriage, arranged when she was twelve. Not unusual for India, but her husband Ashok flaunted the custom and brought street prostitutes to their house.

"I hate him," Padma said fiercely while holding her chai tea. "He treats me like I'm one of his possessions. All he wants is someone to cook and to clean." Then she looked up, startled. "What's got into me? Here I'm telling a complete stranger about my personal problems."

Chandi, smiled tenderly, feeling a thawing of her dark heart. She reached out and patted Padma's hand. "Perhaps you needed to let your feelings out, and who safer than a stranger?"

An expression crossed Padma's face that could have been worry or fear. "I don't think you'll be a stranger for much longer."

There were too many forbidden thoughts and secrets for Chandi to reveal them. Yet, this small intense woman woke something in her, and she knew that they would meet again to talk.

Chandi ended up extending her stay, although she did not like being in India for too long; too much history welled up. Padma was busy during the days, researching and seeking funding. Chandi made her own excuses for being occupied. In the evenings, when it cooled down slightly, they met for dinner and to talk.

Passion seemed to spark from Padma's eyes as she talked about anthropology, ferreting out where traditions began and how they evolved. The air itself seemed to lighten, to be revitalized when her soft, birdlike voice touched it. Chandi felt drawn into her light. The inhumanity that threatened Chandi's world as the years had spun by moved a little farther into dark recesses.

One night, Padma waved her hands about saying, "Even though the heart of their culture is being threatened, the Khasi men insist they want to change the ownership rights. They don't even understand their own traditions."

Chandi replied ironically, "Well, sometimes traditions have gone on for so long that no-one knows how they started or why." She poured a tumbler of imported scotch and passed it to Padma.

Padma curled herself onto the couch and sipped, both her small hands grasping the wide tumbler. "Mmm, this is so good. I love this stuff, but it's so hard to get here." Her eyes held a light that reflected her enjoyment.

Chandi smiled and sat down, crossing her long legs, looking briefly at the full curve of Padma's hips and legs outlined by her thin silk sari. "Well, I'll leave you a bottle when I go back to New York."

A frown clouded Padma's face before she looked down into her drink. Softly, she half-whispered, "You're leaving? I thought..." Padma shook her head, then took a swallow of the oily-looking alcohol, not meeting Chandi's eyes.

"You thought what?" Chandi sat beside her, pulling the soft curling hair back from Padma's downturned face. "Padma?" Her finger brushed Padma's cheek, sending warning flares along her own skin. Padma shuddered and turned to look at Chandi.

Sincerity and scotch added a hint of huskiness to Padma's voice. "I thought ... you liked me."

Warmth, which usually only suffused Chandi when she drank blood sacrifices, melted her resolve to remain apart. Unable to look away from Padma's shiny eyes, she ran her finger down Padma's cheek and throat. "I do. I do very much."

In an interval that was interminably long, yet as quick as their breaths, Chandi's lips brushed Padma's. Tasting slightly of the burnt tones of scotch, Padma's firm, supple kiss answered Chandi's own.

"I like you a great deal, Padma. You're the fire that holds back the night."

Padma sighed into the kiss, sending a butterfly of heat and longing into Chandi's mouth, permeating her with a thrum that electrified her from head to toe. Slowly, Padma leaned back.

"I ... like you very much, Chandi, but I must return home now. It is very late."

Chandi stood, helping Padma to her feet. "I insist in walking you home. I'd hate for anything to happen to you."

Padma smiled shyly, adjusting her burgundy sari. "What about you? You'll have to walk back by yourself."

"True. But I've learned many ... self-defense tactics that have been helpful in New York." She could not yet mention to Padma the real reason she would be safe, if she ever could.

They could have taken one of the many rickshaws or taxis, but neither mentioned it and they moved quietly together. They did not touch as they walked, but their closeness was more than flesh. Padma moved slowly, rolling into each step, her arms crossed, and a small smile flitting over her face, then replaced by a tiny frown.

"Why do you stay with him?"

Padma looked up at Chandi. "Because, we formed a sacred bond."

Chandi couldn't keep all the scorn out of her voice. "Sacred bond? You've told me yourself how much he honors that bond."

"Yes." Padma hesitated then stopped. The warm night air blanketed them in stillness. Chandi had, through the years, come to understand the different nuances of silence. "But I honor the sacredness, the vows we have made. I try to uphold the tradition even if he does not. And I will not stoop to his tactics."

A sigh escaped before Chandi could hold in her exasperation. "That tradition will get you killed. You could come with me to New York."

"I can't."

"For a while, at least. A vacation?"

Padma shook her head. "I can't. Not ... yet. I have to finish my research first. And it's easier to do it here at the source. She began walking again, and they moved in silence until they reached Padma's door.

Chandi's fingers traced the plane of Padma's cheek. "Well, don't rule it out. We can talk further about it. I could help you find funding."

The door flew open. "Where have you been?" demanded the balding man in the doorway. He glared at Padma and pulled her toward the interior. "You never told me you were going out."

"She was with me," replied Chandi calmly. She held out her hand, more to delay Padma's leaving than to actually get to know this man. "I'm Chandi."

He just stared at her until Padma said, "This is Ashok, my husband. I met Chandi at the film festival."

"I don't care. Get inside." He started to push her through the door but she turned to say good night to Chandi. That's when Ashok's meaty palm slapped her face. "I told you, get inside now."

Chandi's hand was around his wrist in an instant. "Don't you dare hit her again."

He wrenched his hand free and snarled, "What I do with my wife is none of your business."

"Yes, it is." She glared down at him and did not move back. "She is a human being and my friend, and she does not deserve your abuse."

"She is my wife." His darkly shadowed gaze did not leave her face. "And you know nothing of what she deserves."

Chandi let some of the hunter flare in her golden tiger's eyes. Ashok started slightly but held his ground. "I know very well what she deserves. Don't hit her again."

Padma pushed in between them. "Ashok, Chandi, it's not enough to fight about. I'm home now, and it's late. Let's go to bed," she said to Ashok and pulled him into the house.

She pointedly looked at Chandi before she went inside. Ashok continued to stare at Chandi but then looked away.

After the door closed Chandi stayed quietly in the shadows for a while, listening for the sounds of fighting. When all remained calm through the hour, she finally left.

Two nights crawled by until Chandi saw Padma again, but she was well and said she had just been busy. Over the next languorous week, they talked and strolled through the brightly lit streets. Though they grew closer, Chandi had done no more than kiss Padma, afraid to dive deeper into the unknown future. Chandi had all the time in the world, but the proximity to the temples of Kali began to weigh on her. It was time to leave.

She tried in vain to persuade Padma to move to New York with her. There were more chances of finding funding there, but Padma refused, not until her research on the documentary was done. It was easier to finish it in India. "It's important to preserve the culture and to make sure certain traditions aren't lost. It should only take another six to eight months," Padma replied.

Her hands splayed out in front of her, and Chandi said, "And what of the tradition that leaves you in Ashok's clutches? It's bad enough that you don't even love him, and even despise him, but that you're still his wife and possession is intolerable. He's beaten you, Padma. He'll continue to do it too. That's where tradition gets you, caged by outmoded ideas."

Padma's lip trembled, but she stubbornly continued, "Weren't you ever married? You said you were born here. Didn't you end up as someone's possession at some point too?"

Chandi bit her tongue, then turned and stared out the murky window that overlooked smog-shrouded Bombay's evening lights. "Yes," she replied. "To Kali."

Taking a deep breath, she turned and looked at Padma. "I have secrets to tell you, but please, don't leave until I'm done."

Padma looked surprised, but only nodded. Chandi bit her lip and wondered why she wanted to open up to this woman. It was partly, she knew, to try and help Padma, but also because there was a strong attraction taking hold. In the incense-laden air, Padma sat quietly and listened, drank her scotch and then poured another. Chandi let everything out, from how she had made her way through the centuries to why she needed Padma. For love, for even one of Kali's dakini needed love.

When she stopped, Padma was still there, and she began to speak so quickly that Chandi could barely answer fast enough. But the words were not the ones she'd been expecting. No, "You've got to be joking," or, "I don't want to see you." No, "Will you kill me now that I know the secret," or, "How could you?" Only, "What was it like?" and, "How did it feel?" and, "What did you see?" and, "But you seem so human."

Sadly, Chandi replied, "I am human, of human blood, but yet so different. Both more and less."

Padma rattled more questions at her until finally, shakily, Chandi held up her hands. "Wait, wait! You mean you're not ... horrified at what I am?" She tried to make light of it, but her mouth pulled down. She still couldn't quite believe that Padma hadn't yet condemned her.

Padma answered, "Horrified? I love you."

Then Padma's fingers unbuttoned Chandi's blouse, and Chandi's hands burrowed beneath Padma's sari. Clothing slithered to the floor. Their lips brushed each other like ephemeral wings brushing the air. Chandi's cool amber skin had broken out in a sweat as Padma's hot tongue trailed shivers down her shoulder and then her thigh. In a cascade of silk, Chandi's fingers revealed Padma's chai-colored skin. Her deep chocolate-colored nipples invited kisses. Chandi worked her way down to the cleft between Padma's legs.

More kisses. Her tongue roved along silken contours till Padma shuddered in her arms. A blending; a marriage of honey and cream. A swirl of love and being one that moved beyond what called Chandi or what drove Padma.

Pulled into a vortex of feeling, Chandi murmured, "You are my light, Padma. You are the fire that drives back the night."

It was morning when Padma left.

That evening, Chandi rose with a smile on her face. She dressed more carefully, slower, feeling the daze of happiness suffuse her. Padma would be with her again tonight.

At a quarter past eight, Chandi began to worry. Padma had wanted to see a movie, a cultural exposé on a small tribe in southern India. She'd talked about it constantly for the past week. Yet, she was now a half-hour late.

Apprehension growing, Chandi disappeared into the softened shadows of evening and moved quickly to Padma's home. She knocked on the stained door. Then she knocked louder. "Padma! I won't leave until you answer." Still no answer, but, when she tried the handle, it gave—with a bit of force.

No lights illuminated the interior, and the furniture mattered little. Chandi didn't need light to see; she moved from room to room until she found Padma laying on the bed and crying softly. Relieved that Padma was at least alive, Chandi hastily made sure that Ashok was not in the house. Then she returned to Padma.

"Pad?" She sat beside Padma and touched her shoulder.

Her muffled voice replied, "Just go, Chandi. Just go."

Gently but firmly Chandi turned her over and swept the hair from in front of Padma's face. Padma's hands flew up, but Chandi held them away and saw what she had expected. "Oh, Padma."

Padma's bruised face shone with tears and blood.

Rage rose quickly, flushing Chandi's heart to molten. She stood and pulled Padma to sitting position. "He'll pay for this." Turning, she went to the chest of drawers and opened drawers until she found Padma's saris and cholis. She started tossing garments on the bed. "Get a suitcase. You're staying with me."

"But I can't."

Chandi snapped, "You can. There is no honored tradition of beating one's wife. He'll kill you if you stay. You know that. And..." Chandi choked up, but went on. "And I have just found you. I will not lose you." She kneeled and gently kissed Padma.

Fiercely they embraced, Padma murmuring into her hair. "He knew I'd been gone all night. I told him I loved you. And I do. I have never loved anyone like I have you, Chandi."

Once they had packed Padma's clothing and papers, they left.

Chandi settled Padma into her apartment knowing that Ashok knew nothing about her or her whereabouts. She fed Padma scotch and bathed her wounds, then put her to bed.

In the middle of the night, Chandi went on the hunt. "Kali, Black Mother, I make you an offering this night."

She picked up his scent from their home, then followed it down the streets and alleys wet with indescribable lumps and oily rivulets. Unsurprisingly, his smell, acrid like souring lentils, led to a brothel. Boldly moving through the ramshackle place, Chandi did not care who saw her. Some might think she was a worker, others would not care or notice.

In a room curtained with a frayed, thin piece of cotton she found him, just getting dressed. He zipped his pants beneath the sagging belly and reached for his shirt. But his hand connected with her arm. Ashok started to laugh, to say, "I thought you'd had enou—" Seeing Chandi, he said, "How did you get here?"

She looked at the prostitute on the bed just rising to protest. "Out."

"But this is my room."

"Out!" Not caring, she confronted Ashok and punched him in the gut. He grunted and crumpled over his ample belly. But Chandi gave him no reprieve and grabbed him by the throat. The prostitute scrambled from her bed and ran from the room, probably for help.

Chandi's hand clamped on Ashok's throat, but he still managed to gasp out, "B-bitch."

Her hand dropped as her other hand came up in a fist and smashed into his face, not as hard as she could have or his face would have caved in. "How does it feel? Do you like this, Ashok? Do you think that Padma has enjoyed the pain you've given her? Have you ever even shown her affection? If you had she may never have needed love elsewhere." She slapped his face twice.

She heard raised voices on the floor below, moving closer.

Ashok gasped out, "Go ahead, kill me. If you do, you'll lose her for sure. That I know."

Several more times, Chandi slapped and punched him, punctuating her words with her hands. "Oh, I won't kill you. You don't deserve such an easy release. But if you ever go near her again, I will." She stopped, in control, not breathing hard. The fear in his eyes made them glitter like black stones.

The voices were outside the room. Chandi said, "Don't ever go near her again." Then she moved in quickly and kneed him hard in the groin. He went down, and she leapt to the window and was gone as the first person entered the room.

Padma was quiet for the first two days, unwilling to talk, but eventually she let her grief and pain out. Chandi soothed her, holding her close. "Padma, I'll stay as long as you need to finish your research. But when you're done, come with me. Please." Chandi bit her lip, wondering how strong Padma's sense of tradition was. Would it keep her in India forever?

Then Padma just nodded, sighing.

Chandi closed her eyes, not daring to speak.

The call came early in the morning, when she was groggiest, already nodding off from her book, and barely able to lift the receiver.

"Padma has honored Sati, as was her right."

"Who is this?" Silence. Chandi looked around the suite, and dread clutched her gut. No sign of Padma. Then she saw the note. Padma had gone home for some forgotten research. "Ashok? What have you done? Where is she?"

"In the hospital. Don't bother going to see her. Let her die in peace. She's mine, not yours."

Fear nearly choked her and made her breathless. "I will get you for this."

She could, too, any time. He just laughed and hung up. For all her words all she could do now was wait until evening and hope Padma still lived. Cursing her limitations, she lay down to sleep.

As the last ray of daylight withdrew, Chandi raced from her door, had in fact already been pacing for hours, waiting until she could leave. In the streets, Chandi heard people shouting and laughing, heard the discordant snatches of music as they celebrated Diwali. Paying little attention, she ran all the way to the hospital, dodging cars, bicycles, and cows.

Bursts of ghostly radiance flickered through the drawn blinds in Padma's room. The lights were dimmed, though Chandi could see well enough. Did the nurses do it to soothe the damaged patient or to lessen the horror for family?

Yet, it was family that had caused this. Ashok stood there blandly staring at Padma's unmoving form. He started at the sight of Chandi at the door. She towered over him, willowy, yet strong as a taut bow. Ashok backed up a step.

Then he shrugged and shook his head. "I told her to be careful. But those kitchen fires, so uncontrollable, and no one was around."

"You. Miserable. Impotent. Worm." She advanced a couple of steps. "You could have just let her go."

"She's mine," he said, and glanced about, sweating heavily in the warm evening air. She could see his bluster falter when he realized that they were alone. "She had no right to leave."

"You didn't want her. You never loved her."

Ashok mustered his courage and flipped his hair out of his eyes, then puffed out his chest. "There's nothing you can do. She was my wife; she'll stay my wife until she's dead. Get out."

Chandi swallowed back her fury, held it in check. "I suggest," she said, letting the fire rage in her voice, "that you leave before you leap from the window in your grief." She moved in close, very quickly, before he knew she had.

She used everything she could to drive in that intimidation, and her tiger's glare made him look away. He tried a laugh that failed. "There's nothing you can do," he repeated, but it was he who left.

And what could she do? In all her years, so many she had lost count, she had never been able to really heal the ill or bring life. She could only bring death. In that, there was little difference between her and Ashok. He too had brought death to Padma, but not merciful, swift, and painless death.

Chandi went over to Padma, who still lived, if a burbling mass of melted skin and hair immersed in a burn tank could be called living. Burns to sixty percent of her body, the nurse had told Chandi in the hall. She could live if she made it through the next twenty-four hours. Whether there would be any life of quality was the question. But there was shock. Shock could kill. Chandi had seen it happen enough times before at her own hands, but please, not to Padma. *Shiva, Kali, please, not Padma.*

It had been a long time since Chandi had manifested Kali, but the urge was strong in her this night. However, nothing she did now could reverse the events that had made Padma a charred, reddened thing. Cherished Padma. Without her, there was little light left for Chandi. And yet, it was light, or rather fire, that had taken everything away.

"What sacrifice, Kali, what sacrifice do you want?" Chandi whispered fervently. No answer, except for the hum and beep of machines that monitored Padma's life systems.

All Chandi could do was get the best care for Padma, a private room, but moving her to another hospital was out of the question. And this, like so many other Indian hospitals, left much to be desired in cleanliness. The walls held indefinable stains, the floors showed the dirt that clung to everything.

Chandi waited, praying, feeling helpless.

The hum and beep of the machines, their neon green and red lights watching, sang an odd counterpoint to the festival of Diwali raging outside.

"Ch-Chan…"

She lifted her head quickly and moved to the burned thing that was Padma. "Pad?" Her hand reached out, but there was no part of the woman that she could touch.

A wet rattle emerged from Padma's lips, then she whispered, "…love you…"

"And I love you, my f—" Chandi choked on saying *fire*; fire had burned away everything good and brought back the night. She chewed her lip fiercely, drawing the sweet, coppery tang of her own blood. Leaning in close, she whispered, "Padma, I can save you. You know I can. I can only do it twice at most—I've never—Padma, let me save you."

For a brief moment Padma's eyes opened and met hers, then they shuttered. "No. That road is yours, not mine..."

Padma faded back into unconsciousness. Chandi's nails bit into the heel of her closed fist. The hum and beep, the shouts and fireworks outside, all faded away. Familiar with silence of all types, she knew this one brought death. Padma was delirious, and she wouldn't thank Chandi, but a life was better than this sort of suffering. Any life. And there were always ways to end it. Chandi leaned closer.

"Isn't she dead yet?" Ashok stood in the doorway, no emotion showing on his pudgy face.

Chandi spun, snarled, and in three quick steps had hauled Ashok by his collar into the room; she shut the door, then pinned him against the wall. "Why?" she gritted out, not much caring if he saw her fangs or not.

Ashok trembled, but his voice was all bravado and scorn. "It was my right," he spat. His shirt pulled taut over his hairy belly. "She's my wife, not yours. She was cheating on me, and with the likes of you."

Chandi twisted his shirt collar a little tighter. He had no idea what the likes of her really were. "You brought home prostitutes. You bruised her. Why?"

He refused to answer. Her hand tightened, and he started thrashing for air. She loosened her grip slightly. The whites of Ashok's eyes showed.

"So I can remarry, alright. It was the only way..."

Chandi threw him to the floor. "It wasn't the only way. There were many other ways. Do not let me see you here again, ever. If I do I'll rip your throat out with my hands."

Ashok scuttled away from Chandi's predator glare. She noticed dawn encroaching then. It was nearly time to leave. Before she did, she bribed the staff to keep Ashok away.

She spent a restless morning trying to sleep and, when that didn't work, got up and tried to read. It ended with Chandi pacing back and forth in the curtain-shrouded apartment, waiting until the sky darkened enough to go out. The heat weighted everything to stillness, as if foreboding pressed upon her shoulders. She would not have left Padma's side at all, had it been possible for her to stay.

What gnawed at her stomach was more than hunger; it was a grief and anger that threatened to consume her. Still, she could not put off any longer that she needed blood. Bombay was a fairly modern city, but there were still temples to Kali throughout and, yes, it was time for a manifestation.

Once it was dark enough, Chandi ventured out. Women in saris as bright as tropical flowers, yet muted by the heavy air, walked through the streets. Men in modern Western dress, and a few in Nehru jackets, strolled along, chewing sweetened betel nut or smoking. Chandi made her way through the crowd to the closest temple, gave the words that admitted her into the innermost chambers.

Through a lattice screen of carved-wood flowers, she saw three goats, washed, garlanded with orange marigolds, and waiting blissfully unaware near the scrubbed marble of the sacrificial arena. Turning away, Chandi dropped her clothes and anointed her brow and limbs. The great Black Mother, Kali Ma, stood before her in sculpted relief. Skulls and limbs beringed Kali's neck; fangs sprouted from a mouth chewing on the entrails of Shiva even as she mounted him. The mother of all, giver of life and the destroyer who devours all things, even time itself. No one escapes her embrace in that final black ocean of creation and blood.

Chandi had often performed the sacrifices for Kali Ma: taking thugs, thieves, and murderers—she had torn out their throats, or beheaded them. She had drunk their blood in dedication to Kali and for her own sustenance. Everything became a part of each other. All would melt back into one in

Kali's embrace. Chandi embodied Kali, and she danced the divine dance.

The ritual chants poured from the sacrificial arena and flooded her ears. She waited and prayed to Kali. Something sparked deep within Chandi's mind—vengeance. Soon, she would bring another to Kali's embrace.

The priests appeared with the bowls of blood. Chandi lifted one and poured, drinking, letting the blood run over her body, a flesh-and-blood image of the Black Mother. When she looked at the priests, even they stepped back from the fire they saw in her eyes. The blood tasted sweet. She was used to its clotting thickness, but there had been times when it was all she had been able to do to gag it down. Now, letting the trance take her, she nearly dropped the bowl. It was removed and another put into her hands. She drank, smeared the blood over her breasts and limbs, and danced.

She danced as if time stretched across a vast expanse of night, for it did. She danced as if wound in the entrails that Kali gnawed, as if spun out and drawn back in again. She danced out the darkness, making the night one with her, knowing that it all came to this, that in the end all returns into the great encircling clasp of Kali Ma's arms. She danced and let the inky despair lap out, touching all in the temple until a great wailing howl rose from its walls. She danced, whirling, twirling, and spinning with the cosmos until she was lost among the stars, the white, grinning skulls, and the flowerbursts of Diwali.

Eventually, there was an awareness of hands reverently sponging and drying her body—dabbing soothing oils upon her skin, wrapping her in soft silk—and a liquid other than blood being brought to her lips and lacing her veins with fire.

She found herself outside the stone temple, people parting around her like water around a river rock. Cleaned and dressed again, she couldn't remember the trance, but that had happened so often before that it mattered little. It mattered only that Kali had not forsaken her because of all

the time she had spent in North America. She had work to
do.

She saw the doctor waiting for her. "Sit down, Miss
Kalidas," he motioned to a chair in a little waiting room. The
walls were a pale shade of greenish gray blended with ageless
dirt. The hospital was one of the better ones in India, but the
halls spoke of neglect and insufficient funds.

Chandi sat and closed her eyes for a moment. Then
she opened them and said, "Is she still alive?"

The clean-shaven man looked down at his watch and
said, "She is, but I'm sorry, we don't expect her to make it.
Her injuries are just too severe. And the shock to her system
has been too much. I'm sorry. We've done what we can to
ease her suffering." He hesitated under her intense gaze, but
added, "If she lived, she would lead a crippling life, always in
pain. It is better this way. I'm sorry."

He left Chandi sitting there, staring at nothing. How
many times had this happened before? Not so many that she
couldn't remember every person she had cared about. Not
many could bear to be with a servant of Kali, or be trusted
with the knowledge of what it meant. As Chandi sat there
letting the darkness swirl in her mind, she knew she had
loved no-one like Padma. Padma completed and
complemented her.

She managed to go to Padma's room; the silence was
such that it was almost as if death had already settled there.
The only sounds were the murmur of machines and their
beeps. Something greater than anger and hunger balled itself
in her stomach and pulled at her throat. Nevertheless,
Chandi moved to Padma's bedside and looked down. There
was a hollow growing inside her. She wanted Padma to live,
to be able to laugh and make love again, but she dared not
pray to any god to let Padma live in the state she was. If she
lived she would be crippled and in pain until she died. Yet,

Padma knew Chandi could save her. The cost would be dear, but she would heal.

Chandi found herself gnawing her knuckles. Wetness slipped over her cheeks, and she realized that she was crying—something she had not done since she was a young girl, freshly dedicated to the sect of Kali. She reached forward, determined now to give Padma the kiss of life. Chandi was not sure she could live without her.

A sudden change in Padma's breathing halted Chandi. "Padma," she whispered softly. And Chandi hesitated. Could she stand the anger, perhaps the hatred, Padma would have for her if she lived through Chandi's touch?

"Chandi." It was like a long sigh. Padma's eyes didn't open.

"I love you, Padma."

"Chan—don't kill..." The words were barely more than exhalations. Chandi leaned as close as she could, thankful for her heightened hearing.

"Don't kill? Padma, I must—"

"No. Ashok."

Chandi had misunderstood; she wanted to scream at Padma, "You won't let me heal you, and now you take away my vengeance too," but she didn't. In the long run, Padma would not know what Chandi did.

"Promise."

It was hard to get the words around the lump that blocked her throat. A sob escaped before she nodded her head and said, "I promise, Pad." She blurted out, "Please let me save you. Please. I need you."

"No."

Chandi cried but Padma would not change her mind. Then Chandi noticed her breathing deepening. "Padma, please don't go..."

"Love you..." A long sigh escaped her and no more. Kali Ma had welcomed Padma home.

Chandi turned away, consumed by tears she could not hold back, feeling as if the darkness would swallow her until she disappeared.

It was the darkest part of night. Nothing stirred; even the ever-present rats seemed to be sleeping. The warm night air held no breeze, and everything seemed to hold its breath, waiting for the light, or for a cool wind. Soon the monsoons would begin.

Neither insects nor cats heard her move into Ashok's house, glide over broken floorboards, around sparse furniture, and into the bedroom. She was sitting on his chest before he woke, her other hand covering the mouth of the woman sleeping beside him. The woman struggled and beat at Chandi's hand but could not remove it. Ashok woke with a start and a muffled shriek at Chandi's cool hand around his throat. The whites of his eyes shone brightly in the room.

"She's dead," she growled, "because of your pettiness and greed." Her hand tightened on his throat until he gagged.

Chandi lowered her face within an inch of Ashok's. The woman beside him stopped moving, her body trembling. Chandi's fangs gleamed in the sickle moon's light, which bled through the curtains. "You are lower than a worm, for a worm is still part of this Earth. I am Chandi Kalidas; know that name, for it is your fate. I am a dakini, and you have provoked the Black Mother's wrath. Some day I will strike you down like the rat you are, but you will not know when, you will not know where." She slid one sharp nail an inch along his neck, opening a fine cut from which blood trickled. Her fingertip dipped in the blood and she raised it to her mouth, then spat it out in his face. "Even your blood is sour. I'll be watching you, Ashok." She smelled the sharp tang of his urine, and smiled. "You will not know when, but you [will] feel Kali Ma tear into your entrails and you will feel every bite."

She left as silently as she had appeared. It would be a long while before he or the woman dared to even move from their bed.

Some day when she felt that her promise to Padma had been fulfilled, that Ashok had lived in terror long enough, she would sacrifice his blood to Kali. For now, she would honor Padma's last wish.

Her body was wrapped in the sacred saffron-colored shroud, marigolds adorning her bier like bright eyes in the dark. They carried her body through the streets, torches lighting the way. People moved out of their path, or disappeared, not wanting to be part of the funereal atmosphere in the last days of Diwali, the festival of lights. They wound up the hill to the burning ghats. There, everyone departed, friends and family, except for the priests who would preside over the cremation. Chandi stayed and none dared remove her, for she wore the blood-red and black robes of a devotee of Kali.

She watched as the priests chanted, and as they slid Padma into the purifying fire. Like a phoenix she would be reborn, and maybe Chandi would be lucky enough to recognize her in her new incarnation.

As the flames licked up the marigolds and began to devour the shroud, tears wetted Chandi's face. She never moved throughout the cremation. Padma's body disappeared, enveloped by red and yellow flames and by white-hot tongues of heat.

Chandi whispered, "You are the fire that holds back the night.

THE BOY WHO BLED RUBIES

Writing as T. C. Calligari

I picked the last lock in the hall and saw the boy…the young man, a reclining amber statue on a divan while his wrist dripped slow red blossoms onto glass. Mesmerized by the blood blooming into crystals, I let my guard down. Ruby crystals.

Gray metal, guards in mail obliterated the image of the red jewels, much like the ones in the sack I held. They strode from two elaborate, blue marbled corridors. Cornered at the end of one, I turned back the way I had come to the T, to the door I had first picked. More guards clustered at the exits. I had but two choices; to fight my way through them or be trapped with that strange scenario behind the golden door.

I swung the sack of gilt, gem-encrusted candlesticks, ruby sculptures and ornate miniatures of the rulers into the three approaching guards, then spun and backflipped. Running at the other two guards, I stepped up one from knee to shoulder, and then propelled myself toward freedom.

It was in sight when a strong hand whipped out and grabbed my ankle, slamming me to the floor. I managed to blunt the impact with my hands, and rolling face up I prepared to kick out, when a fist thumped the side of my head. Black washed over me.

I had always lusted for the finer things in life, and it had nearly landed me in trouble, except I had been too good. Up until now. I came to in a room, opulent, but furnished oddly. Thirty-foot walls held carved, golden framed paintings of sumptuous landscapes placed well out of the reach of a man, even if standing on a chair. Chairs there were, but overstuffed, soft constructs. An extremely sturdy and thick-legged table stood to one side, looking out of place and utilitarian. The other furnishings and the bed were equally padded or so heavy it would have taken several strong men to move them.

I had been tossed onto a carmine carpeted floor and stood, realizing I was naked. The boy who had been bled sat upon a chair near the door and I stopped. His skin glowed amber, gold flecks showing from deep umber eyes, black glossy hair in a tousle of curls against his green and gold brocade collar. He had lost the rounded softness of childhood and now showed the harder planes of a man, but boy he was to me. He looked me over, possibly seeing a naked man in his prime for the first time. I had never seen features more perfect on any man or woman, and I had been with a great number of nearly perfect women, though none had held my interest for long. Like all treasures, they pale against the ones not yet attained. This boy would be able to rule anyone just by bestowing a favored glance. Many a person would do anything to be in his presence. But not me. I would see if he served me any purpose.

After an appraising look at my muscled, finely haired chest down to my sinewy legs, he pointed with his chin. "There are clothes for you over on that chair."

Perhaps I stared too long before I turned, for he softly said, "They tell me I am handsome, one of the most beautiful in the kingdom."

"They?"

"The Lock," he replied, but at the shake of my head he elaborated. "The guards and staff who…protect me."

"And you are?"

"I am the Key."

I pulled on the hose and pants, aware he watched me

dress. Everything he said seemed to open up a new cask of questions. "The key. I suppose you're in charge of those you call the Lock."

"No."

I turned and looked at him.

"They are the Lock that protects and holds me; I am the Key to the kingdom."

I stopped. "You're the Key to the kingdom? What do you mean?"

His head tilted, a slight smile gracing his perfect features. "You saw but you still don't know, do you? And yet, your life is forfeit because of it." He shrugged. "Well, no matter. I supply the ruby kingdom its wealth." At my puzzled expression, he sighed. "The rubies come from me. When I bleed my blood turns to rubies."

Rubies, the lifeblood of the kingdom. I remembered what I'd seen as I picked up a fine linen shirt with high collar and an accent of lace. "Do you not have a more personal name then? It is hard for me to call you the Key." I fastened the abalone buttons on the shirt and tied it at the neck. My captors had guessed my size well, but then they'd had my other clothes, and my tools. As I turned, he stared. I was usually the one to give such appraising looks.

One side of his mouth crinkled and he replied, "I'm rarely called anything else, but my nurse used to call me Uilliam." He gazed into the depth of the carpet. "I suppose she met her end like all the others."

"What others?" I paced the room, checking the walls for windows, under the bed, the weighty drawers, eventually getting to the door and trying the latch.

"It is unlocked. You will find the corridor and rooms beyond open but you will not get past the end of the hall, nor the guards who watch that door day and night. You got through a service entrance. A…lucky break, but they won't make that mistake twice."

"What about the others?" I already knew but wanted the confirmation.

He sighed and came over to me, standing close. A whiff of spice, cinnamon and pepper touched my nose. "When they served their purpose and were no longer needed, they were given their freedom. That's what the Lock calls it but it is a freedom from life, for none who know of me can let my presence be known."

I like puzzles. It's partly why I tired woman after woman, and why I became a thief, defeating obstacles to reach the treasure. Sometimes the journey is more enjoyable than the prize. However, Uilliam was more of a puzzle than I yet had clues or possibly time to solve.

I pulled on soft-soled shoes and turned to Uilliam. "Well, if my time is short, walk with me while I explore. How did you come to be here?"

"And you can tell me about yourself," he said with a solemn look upon his perfect face. "After all, when you cease to please me they will give you your freedom."

I frowned. Surely one so closeted had no idea of worldly pleasures.

|"But," he paused with the most delicate indication of a frown kissing a brow so smooth I nearly touched it. "Even if you entertain me, you only have a limited number of days. The Lock is very efficient."

I laughed. "And I have never found a lock I could not open."

We walked down a hall with gilt framed doorways. The marble floors and pillars were like moonstone, and luxurious patterned carpets displayed all manner of beast and flower. The paintings gracing the walls depicted fantastical lands and animals, only the odd one a portrait.

"That one," Uilliam pointed to his right, his lace cuff falling back to show a bandage wrapping his wrist, "is the grandsire of Cairbre. It was Gonal who first found my mother."

I tried the doors along the hall. Some were locked and others identical to the one we had left. "Did she bleed rubies too?"

"No." He shook his head, black curls tumbling about his eyes. "I am the only one. You have not told me your name."

I cocked an eyebrow at him. "If I tell you, then when I escape you will have a name to give the Lock."

He stopped and laid a hand upon his chest. It drew my eye to the pulse at his neck. "I give you my word on my mother's grave, I will not reveal your name…if you escape."

Opening a door, I entered another room with a glass ceiling. I called back to him as he peered after me. "They call me Palae." Outside I could see trees but none that branched near the solarium windows.

"Why do you steal?" he asked.

"Because I can." There was nothing in this room I could break; no stand, mirror, flasks, urns, plants: just large overstuffed furniture of leviathan weight. I left.

He paused, then followed. "But why? They tell me the kingdom is wealthy and no one wants. It is the service I provide." He glanced at me but I just smiled and shrugged. He held out his hand. "Come, I'll show you the most interesting rooms, not that there are many. I could walk them in the dark and have often enough."

I hesitated, feeling too drawn to this unusual young man. He was a most unique treasure, after all. "How long have you been here?"

"All my life; eighteen or more years. I have known no other place," he said without emotion.

"I notice no pottery, plants or animals."

"No." He glanced over his shoulder and turned right down a hall. "They can cut, or scratch or poison or bite. None can hurt me except those who bleed me for rubies. The kingdom depends on me."

I moved in menacingly. "What is to stop me from killing you with my hands or using you to bargain my way out of here?" And I would, if he served my purpose.

His shrug was an elegant shift of lace as he stepped closer and looked me in the eye. "They would not let you take me." His lips quirked. "They would kill you either way, and me if there was no choice. You still have not said why you steal."

I turned and tapped the walls, then checked the floor. There was no nail, no splinter of wood anywhere, no shard of glass with which I could hurt Uilliam or myself. This was indeed a gilded cage. "I steal because there is no place that is perfect. Yes, the Ruby Kingdom provides for its citizens, if they toe the line. I steal to challenge the rules."

We walked in silence until we reached the end of the hall. The door was locked and he said it led beyond the Lock's realm, where he had never been. He opened the door to the left. It was like walking into a golden tomb, muffled with rows on rows of leather-bound books, their embossed covers as bright as birds' feathers. The gold winked in the torchlight like knowing eyes. Yet again the sconces were beyond reach, away from the books and the walls.

Night had fallen, and as I turned in the room I saw a woman using a long wand with a taper at the end to light the last torch. Two guards walked with her. One watched her and the other watched us, especially me.

"Good evening, Master," said the shaven headed Lock guard.

"Good evening, Bors," replied Uilliam. "Tell the cook to send our dinner here."

Bors nodded.

Curious, I walked toward the woman, who glanced at me in fright. Broad shouldered and strong browed Bors moved between us.

"You may not approach."

"Why?"

"It could cause harm."

I smiled. They'd bested me once but I thought I was faster. This was not the time, for I had nowhere to run. I bowed my head and turned away, realizing that the maid, as well as the Lock and any others, were as caged as Uilliam. There was only one way to leave service to the Key, and I would not willingly choose it.

As the guards and maid left, Uilliam pulled several books from the shelves and settled into a chair of plush amber. I sat across from him.

"This room lacks a fireplace. The season is warm but how do they heat your rooms in winter?"

He flipped idly through a book, motions as graceful as any dancer. "There are fires in the grates of the floor below this one. They feed the heat up through the flues. If you look carefully, you will see the vents, well covered in thick iron. There is no escape through them. I tried."

I gazed thoughtfully at him and he shrugged. "You look like someone who has seen much of the world." He held up a book. "This is my world, the only one I've ever known. I have only glimpsed the sky and an odd tree through the solarium. I have never seen an animal that was not served on my plate. I have never felt the grass beneath my feet or breathed the outside air. I have never known a friend who could stay, who wasn't judged as a threat to my health.

"I eat well, healthier possibly than Cairbre and Dellmona. I'm not allowed to overindulge for it could make me ill. I am given exercise, enough to keep me vital, and filtered sunlight but nothing can jeopardize me. The finest jewel in the kingdom has a better life for at least it is taken out and admired. Not even the rulers come to see me," he finished.

"No?" I wondered at his calmness. Was it from acceptance or having no hope?

"No." A flush colored his cheeks to darker amber. "No, for though they say it is for my protection, they fear their guilt would get the better of their greed, and their greed is ultimate," he replied between clenched teeth. "My blood flows though I have no life."

"And mine will soon end," I added, "though I wager I've had more of a life than you."

"Yes."

At that point the same maid brought in our meal. Two thick, wooden platters laid out with vegetables, a mound of already cut meat and potatoes. Two wooden cups and a pitcher holding pomegranate juice, another holding water. All the implements were wooden. She left with the guard.

We left off conversation to eat. Uilliam warned me as I turned over the fork in my hand, barely sharp enough to skewer the meat. "Don't think of pocketing any. The Lock has counted all pieces and expects the same number back, and whole."

When we were done, the maid took away all but the pitchers and the cups.

"Are you content?"

He laughed but there was no humor. "I cannot leave, I cannot die, and they will surely bleed me regularly until the end of my days."

I still hoped to discover a way out. The Lock was very efficient, but all humans make mistakes "How does your blood turn to ruby?"

"When it hits the air, it crystallizes. That's all I know. Sometimes they bleed me into a mold to make the sculptures. Sometimes they leave it for the artisans to carve."

"Tell me, Uilliam, what is it you most desire?"

It was as if the books, his only friends for so long, held silent to hear his words. Uilliam played with a curl against his cheek. He was amazing to watch, each movement like a god's. After a long while, he said, "I desire life, true life. I am used to the cut of an obsidian blade, but to feel the sun even if it would blister me, to be truly thirsty or hungry, to know the sensation of touching nature at its wildest even if a beast tore off my arm. If only I could feel life, just once, I would be content to die."

"Would you risk your life to escape?"

His eyes flashed and he stared at me. Slowly he brought an elegant finger to his lips. "Come over here. I want to show you a book."

We moved to the cloistered nook where numerous volumes lined three walls. He grabbed a book and sat down, with me peering over his shoulder. He was so perfect I had to still my impulse to touch him. "Here, see." As I leaned down he said, "It is impossible. Others have tried and met the Lock's clasp."

I whispered over his shoulder, inhaling the scent of his hair, "I know. The Lock is dangerous but with the right tool I can open anything." I did not say that he would be that tool. "I have nothing to lose, as I will be dead one way or another soon. How long do I have?"

"A week at most."

"Then I will take the chance. But you, you will lose the safety and sanctity and may in the end gain nothing but the freedom the Lock gives."

"I would take death rather than live this stagnant life a second longer."

I kneeled beside his chair and stared up at him. "Then show me what you bleed."

He shook his head. "I cannot. They use a very fine blade and apply a salve that would be the envy of any chirurgeon. Already the wound is growing closed."

"Then we shall make another." I produced a small sliver of bone from my dinner. His eyes widened, then narrowed. It was not big enough to do much damage. I grabbed his finger, and pricked it with the pointed edge of bone. He gasped and I squeezed until a droplet welled up.

I saw nothing at first and blinked from the intensity of staring. When I looked closer it seemed the light faceted off the drop.

"Not yet," he said, and gently pried my hand from his finger. He held it up to the light and turned his finger back and forth. Finally, he said, "Here," and reached up with his other hand, breaking off the tiny pearl of red. He dropped it in my open palm.

It was indeed the tiniest globe of ruby, perfect for a ring or an earring, worth at least three gold sovereigns unmounted. I pocketed it and the bone. "We will work with what we have, but now I need a good night's sleep."

It had been a long day. Perhaps, when faced with our eminent mortality time does slow down. It gave me time to think, to plan and to dare hope. I knew how to sleep through the toughest situations, but my thoughts burned with images of Uilliam late into the night. He would indeed help me unlock the prison, but after that, I would not need him and he was too inexperienced to survive the world.

In the morning, Uilliam and I ate, then we went to the library where the muffled histories kept prying ears at bay.

"Tell me," I asked as I leafed through some old, ornately tooled tomes, "how often do they bleed you?"

He shrugged, glancing up from an illuminated page that depicted palm trees and camels. "It depends. If they wish to make a large piece then I'm bled, and left alone for a week or two. If it's smaller, I might be bled every day for a week before I get a rest."

"Don't your arms get sore?"

"Not really." He smiled at me. "I suppose if I were a farmer working in the fields that the plow would bother me little after a while. They try not to scar me much and the salve helps a great deal, but they are careful to map where they have cut and then cut higher and lower so the same place is not visited more than three or four times in a year. See."

He rolled his sleeve up to his elbow. The bandage of yesterday was gone and his wrist bore a faint pink scar. A few light lines graced his arms but overall they were hardly marred.

"Impressive. How do they keep you from weakening with continual blood loss?"

"A great deal of meat. I've come to accept it in its less cooked state."

Although we'd had fowl the previous evening, the portions had been very generous.. At that point I moved closer and showed him a book. "I have been to these lands. They're beautiful, especially under a full moon." And under my breath, I added, "And when will they bleed you next?"

"Not before you're…gone. They don't like others to know and what you saw yesterday was fairly extensive. I need time to regain my strength."

I pulled out the sliver of bone and held it up before my eye. "Your Lock is good but not perfect. This will be the means of our liberation," I whispered. "Now, give me your hand. We need a little blood."

He held his hand out as I kneeled beside him. I grasped the finger and quickly stabbed it, squeezing to get blood to well up. As it did, I drew it out along his finger. Uilliam gasped again, leaning his head back into the velvet cushions and closing his eyes. When the blood had crystallized, I picked up the translucent red needle and said, "Now we make a bigger blade. Are you ready?"

Uilliam nodded and rolled back his sleeve to his elbow. I took the thin ruby glass with its sharp edges and drew it over his forearm. I let the blood well up thickly, making sure to keep a thin edge to one side. Uilliam moaned, his lips parted and his breath came quicker. Once the blood had crystallized, a matter of few minutes, I peeled it off of his arm and recut.

He writhed, his back arching up as he grabbed me with his free hand. At first I thought it was the pain, but he pulled me to him, the firm resilience of his lips crushing into mine. My breath caught and I could not escape noticing the growing bulge in his pants. Disconcerted, I returned his kiss, then quickly broke off. Looking down, I didn't know what to do but continue making the blades. His hand clasped my arm tightly as his neck arched. I looked away.

We finished four ruby blades that I carefully stowed along the inside seams of my waistcoat.

I adjusted my plan at that point. "Tonight, when they think we're asleep, you and I will begin our work. We won't leave till tomorrow. If there's anything you wish to take with you, plan now. Otherwise, let's spend this day with you learning a few of my tricks."

He smiled at me and moved closer for a moment. "I'd like that."

We took off our coats, and in shirts and pants I showed him flips and leaps and how to use a wall or a chair to gain momentum and height. Backflips and cartwheels, handstands and twists, we worked in tandem like acrobats. Uilliam was as much a natural athlete as he was a perfect specimen of humankind.

Throughout the morning we practiced, laughing when the other fell in a ridiculous heap. We broke only for a sip of water or juice until lunch arrived. We ate heartily.

"How's your arm?" I asked, suddenly feeling awkward with conversation.

"Fine. It will heal before long and I have some salve in my bedroom."

"Good." I hesitated, then went with my original idea. "That's where we're off to next." Louder, I said, "All the tumbling and acrobatics wore me out. I think I'll take a nap before this evening."

Uillaim stood, buttoning down his sleeve, giving me a sideways glance. "I'm tired too."

We walked down the hall, but I could think of nothing to say. When we reached his room, he stepped inside. I held my finger to my lips and looked around. No sight of guards. I stretched widely, my back to the door through which the Lock came, and motioned Uilliam to scoot in front of me down to my room. Once he'd entered the room I joined him.

We waited quietly for ten minutes, making sure that the guards were not coming. He stood close and the perfume of his sweat was sweet. I didn't touch him but leaned into his scent.

Carefully, I removed the blades and laid them on a chest, then strode to the bed and pulled off the sheets. "I hope these aren't old linens because our lives will depend on it. Keep an ear to the door."

I looked up to the far windows, gauging their distance, then started cutting six-inch strips of cloth. It was a moment before I realized he stood behind me. I turned and Uilliam's hand came up behind my head, pulling me into a kiss. I've always been the instigator but as his tongue probed over my lips I felt myself respond. My heart hammered my chest as he pulled my shirt open, his fingers trailing fire over my torso. Gasping, I pushed back.

"We don't have time for this." I was afraid. Was I this type of man? I thought I had been using him but a hunger grew in me.

He smiled languidly and pulled his shirt over his head. "What other time but now? I wonder what I could steal of yours, Palae, to challenge your rules."

He peeled out of his pants and moved toward me, naked and perfect, his cock proudly erect. Did I really want him, but I only had to pay attention to my body to know he was a new treasure that I desired. In for a penny, in for a pound, and thieves are always in for a pound.

I reached out to him. Our chests touched, our lips exploring neck and limb, and as we tasted each other I knew, knew that here was wealth I would fight for. We fell into a nest of sheets and torn fabric, entangled in warm limbs. His tongue swirled over my nipples, a light nip, startling me and making my cock jerk in anticipation.

As his lips played over my body I found I could not keep my hands off him, feeling, tweaking, scratching lightly every muscled part of him. Indeed, there were many ways to make him bleed with teeth and nails but it was ecstasy we both sought. We curled like a nautilus about each other and as I explored with tongue and lips the first cock I had ever tasted, he drew me into his mouth. The heat of his cock slid over my tongue, filling me as his hands cupped and gently squeezed my balls. I groaned and thrust my hips forward. This was not the slow lovemaking of people with infinite time, but the frenzied coupling of hunger and greed. I was as greedy as the rulers for this key and he was unlocking new passages to pleasure within me.

As I came I groaned and gritted my teeth, unwilling to alert the Lock. Uilliam came in my arms, our salty come and sweat making us as slippery as dolphins.

We lay in each other's arms for a few moments. I kissed him and pondered. Treasure and adventure is what I always have sought, to stifle an inner boredom, a want I could not fill. Was I willing to risk all I had become for a man like Uilliam?

Perhaps, but not right now. I pushed myself up on an elbow and stared down at him. "Time to get back to work."

He eyed the strips of cloth I picked up and shook his head. "We still could not reach the windows."

Smiling, I winked as I tied the sheets together. "Just wait, you'll see. A strong throwing arm always helps. Now, go and sleep, be ready for this evening. We're not waiting."

I awoke to a tap on the door and one of the Lock opening it, a wraithlike glow behind him. It took a moment for me to realize it was the maid lighting the sconces for the evening. And that made me remember we had another problem. The Lock would come around to snuff the sconces at evening's end and we'd have to work in darkness. I lay in bed and memorized details. Last night the moon had added enough light. It would be our only guide.

As I waited for the Lock and maid to leave I realized I had never once thought of leaving Uilliam behind. He'd become part of the plan from the beginning. Could a thief ever leave the most beautiful object ever found? Of course, without his ruby blood I couldn't have made the rope, but it was the thought of being caged like a bird for all his days, with few pleasures, that convinced me his freedom was worth the risk. And the risk would be increased a hundredfold when Cairbre and Dellmona found their source of income gone.

Later, after the lights were extinguished, my door opened quietly and Uilliam entered, simply dressed in breeches and shirt, with a coat on his arm. He came over to where I worked, understanding that we had to get the cloth rope first over the sconce and then once one of us had scaled the tied rags, to break the glass with a wrapped arm and toss the linen rope out the window. Then we'd drop down the outside of the building. A risk, but he had risked kissing me, not knowing how I would react.

"Palae." His hand stroked my face and I groaned, my cock stiffening at his touch. He leaned in and kissed me. I answered with the pressing warmth of my own kiss. His tongue slid like silk over my lips, exploring my mouth.

I had always been a doer, a seeker, adventuring out so I didn't have to venture within. I had made myself in the image I wanted to be, just as Uilliam had been made to be the Key. He had unlocked a part of me I hadn't known was hidden. The missing pieces, the discontent fell away to reveal my fascination with this boy who bled rubies, yet who was a man, wise and caged. I had been seduced by beauty. Again.

I adjusted myself, then put my hands on his shoulders. "It's all or nothing now."

He smiled as he took the rope, ran off the bed and into my hands, which boosted him enough to get the rope over the fixture. As he fell back I caught him. We smiled at each other and began the great climb out.

Once we were on the run, it would be the first adventure that I had taken with complete seriousness. Many would covet Uilliam even if they did not know who or what he was. He had given me the greatest treasure of the kingdom and it wasn't rubies. He was its lifeblood as he was mine. Once set free, neither of us could be caged again. I was willing to take the chance and would protect him and fight for him, maybe even die for him. But isn't that what love is always about?

A KIND HAND

It wasn't unusual that Berchta flayed babies and ate them. Or so the superstitious said. Strange thoughts for Andreas, to be sure, but it had all started with the suspicious mumbling at the tavern. After all, she seemed to skin everything, turning it into inside and outside, seeing to the marrow of the matter.

Andreas pulled his coat tight against the icy fingered wind and squinted through the light tumble of snowflakes as he trudged his way home. Not that he believed such rumors. She was only a woman; that was all.

He had watched Berchta one day when she had come to town. She ate in the tavern, alone, silent. No one sat too near her tall, lean figure hunched over her meat pie like a carrion bird. She wasn't old but seemed ageless, white skin smooth, but not plump with youthfulness. Her hair seemed as pale as her skin, yet Andreas had seen the sun fire color into it, as if it reflected the world around her.

He had leaned back on the bench, slouching slightly and nursing his amber ale. Slyly he had watched as Berchta pulled back the crust of her meat pie, deftly flicking it aside with the sharp shiny blade of her knife. Then she scooped up the glistening brown gravy with a spoon and fastidiously ate it all before she worked on the crust. She had looked up then and straight at Andreas, and a shiver had run down his spine.

He didn't despise her like some of the others. She was quiet and a bit strange, but that was no reason to hate or to build fantastic tales about her. Still, he knew better than to get too near her flinty gaze that seemed to carve away the flesh that covered a man's soul. And she was quick-eared, sharp as a steel blade, hearing a whisper at fifty paces. Such had been the case that time when Bertrand, plump with a rich life, had turned from his stall of walnuts and pecans to wink at Jano and whisper as she passed, "Watch out for Berchta. She's bones with no meat and she'll shrivel your manhood."

Bertrand shut his mouth quickly when Berchta walked up to his stall and plucked up a walnut. She held the hard brown nut up to her eyes, and said, "What do you, good man Bertrand, hide within the shell of your house? Is it that you rip and beat the flesh within for only being flesh when it is the meat within your own nuts that is rancid?" The marrow of the matter.

Shocked to silence by the flaying of her words, Bertrand could only gape and turn purple.

It was true that that winter when Berchta came through the town admonishing those who had not filled their barns with fresh hay, or cleaned hearths and homes properly, that she had spent a longer time at Bertrand's home. But Bertrand's home already suffered. Filled with fever and illness, it was his most loved son that was taken first. And through that last winter his cattle had sickened and dropped one by one, bringing him close to ruin.

No one spoke openly of the ill that befell a slovenly or ill-prepared household after Berchta saw the interior. Where she lived none knew and she frequented the town more in winter than the high heat of summer, warning people to stay home and tend their hearths well every Epiphany eve.

When spring next came and Berchta again walked through the town, Bertrand had no twinkle in his eye and hung his head when she drew near. Even when the pious Horst quietly suggested Berchta was a witch, Bertrand only shrugged and sadly turned back to his stall.

Andreas shook his head at such musings. He huddled into his coat as he walked along the forest path. The biting, icy wind came from the mountains early this year. There'd be more snow before All Hallow's Eve. The root vegetables and squashes had just been gathered this week and the hay brought in to the barns. Berchta had already been warning the townsfolk of a long winter. He'd made sure to help Gerta bring the food in after the cattle were fed that morning. She'd been busy sewing new coats for the two little ones. Gerta always followed what Berchta advised, using spindles free of slivers, weaving tight linen cloth from flax that Andreas had traded for, and cleaning the hearth before the solstice. After all, Gerta had said, "What she says is common sense and gives us better quality."

The pale yellow of the cottage's thatch came into view and Andreas picked up his pace through the cold's reaching fingers that poked under his coat. He had to admit that though he did not believe any of the gossip of the townsfolk about Berchta, still she held some power over them. They minded her words for the most part and did what they could to appease her stern counsel. She was a mystery, showing up every few weeks to trade linen or spindles for food. Perhaps she was a bit nosey, but she was also more tuned to the turning seasons than many.

Andreas shook his head, smiling as he reached for the latch of the door. The warmth and light of the cottage, armed like stolid warriors, pushed the cold back to its outer realm and Andreas entered. "Hello, my little ones," he called out and his girls of four and six bounded to him.

"Papa, Papa," squealed Ingrid. The youngest flung herself against his legs. "Did you see the snowflakes? Will we make snowmen?"

Andreas bent and kissed Hilda's cheek and hefted Ingrid into his arms. "Perhaps my sweet, but I think we won't have that much snow for a while yet." He leaned over to kiss Gerta as she set a dish upon the table, the savory aromas of garlic and rosemary causing his stomach to grumble.

She returned his kiss but smiled sadly. Andreas raised his eyebrows, but Gerta just mouthed "later" over their children's heads.

After dinner, and a short tale for the children, Andreas tucked them into their beds, kissed their foreheads and blew out the lamp. He quietly shut the door.

"I'm just going to check the barn," he told Gerta while she finished putting the dishes away.

He pulled on his coat and took a lantern out to the yard. The air scratched at his lungs, telling him it would be too cold to snow tonight. Overhead the stars glinted like shards of ice. Walking through the steam of his breath, he checked the latches on the barn and the coop, making sure the animals were settled. When he returned to the cottage, he blew on his hands. "I think Berchta is right and we're in for a hard winter."

Gerta sat by the fire, mending Ingrid's shift. "I know. We'll have to stock plenty of wood. When you're next in town, see if anyone has any good wool. Hilda's growing out of her coat already."

Andreas sat down beside his wife, her solid presence and scent of cinnamon and apples always a comfort to him. He put an arm around her shoulder and squeezed. "Now, tell me what's bothering you."

She looked down at her needlework as she said, "Yelena and Nil's son, Jurgen died today. He took a fever yesterday and was gone before they could bring in the doctor."

"Ahh." Andreas felt saddened. "That explains why there was grumbling about Berchta in town. I presume there are those who think she brought the fever."

"Yes, it's a sad thing. Unexplained illness and they blame the one they don't know." Gerta shook her head and looked at Andreas. "I abide by Berchta's wisdom. There is somewhat otherworldly about her and I fear that we may offend what we no longer understand."

"I'd wager there is more wisdom in Berchta than half the townsfolk put together. She has a sharp eye, that one." Andreas kissed Gerta long and passionately. "Well, I'm for bed. There's a lot still to do if we're in for an early winter."

Two days past All Hallows the storm howled in, snowflakes dancing in mad clusters. Andreas checked the animals. Through the blizzard Hilda and Ingrid watched the snow fall, steaming up the thick glass window. But by the time even the sun bedded down from the cold, the moaning and rattling of shutters, now closed against the night, had them clinging to their parents.

Gerta looked over Hilda's head to Andreas. "I think this one night Ingrid and Hilda can share our bed to keep us all warm. It's a fierce storm but we'll be fine."

Andreas gathered Ingrid up in his arms. "We're more than fine. We have a sturdy home and all the cows and chickens are tucked in their beds. Now we'll tuck you two into ours. And when the storm is done, we'll be able to build snowmen."

"Papa?" asked Hilda. "Can the snowmen hurt us?"

Andreas laughed as he put her sister into the bed and Hilda climbed up beside her. Her flaxen hair glowed in the light and Andreas patted her head. "No, sweetheart. We make them but they are only made of snow. Storms and cold can hurt us and that's why we always take care to dress warmly and take food when we travel. Now, your mother will tell you a tale and we'll be to bed soon."

"Papa," Hilda whispered. "Will the storm witch eat us?"

Gerta entered then, as Andreas stood there, wondering where Hilda had got such thoughts.

"Now, Hilda, that is just your imagination. It is only cold and wind and snow. If we keep ourselves warm, we'll be fine." Gerta glanced at Andreas and sat beside the girls.

Andreas entered the sitting room and turned down the lamps. For a moment, he cracked the door and looked out. Flurries of snow spun and twirled as if embodied with wild sprites that had no care of human frailties. He shivered and scratched at his short beard. Winter had no thought behind it but it did sometimes feel as if it directed malign glee at the farmers.

In the morning, the snow still fell but it was a light powdering. Andreas opened the door after breaking his fast and went to clear a path to the barn. The sky was a flat pewter dish, giving an eerie light in the muffled silence. As he shoveled through to the barn, Andreas knew he still had to lay in more wood. The snow was just below his knees and more would follow in the coming months.

He fed the cows and two horses, then cleared a path to the coop so that Gerta could get the eggs. Then he gathered up the snowshoes and tools and went inside. Ingrid's were almost done.

When he entered the cottage, Ingrid looked up from her eggs, bright eyed. "Can we build snowmen today, Papa?"

"Well, my little bunny, we'll build snowmen tomorrow. It's still snowing and the snow will be better for waiting a day. Now I'm going to finish your snowshoes so we can go for walks."

As he twisted the sinew strands, Andreas thought of the repairs he could do when the cold and snow held them cloistered. There were always harnesses to mend, blades to sharpen and wooden items to whittle, especially before Epiphany.

Through the following weeks, Andreas helped the girls build snowmen and other fanciful shapes; one day the whole family began a battle with snowballs and short walls of shored up snow. The weather, having let out its fury, had calmed again. Still cold, the sky held a deep, brittle blue and the sun seemed a pale thing of little light. Ingrid and Hilda grew comfortable on their snowshoes and one day Andreas and Gerta took the girls to town.

It was a fair week with crafts and items from artisans of neighboring villages. Andreas had several blades tucked in an oiled cloth, and wedged on top were some eggs and gourds for trade. Gerta carried a smaller basket with food and tinder, should they need it.

The girls' short gaits slowed their walk. They stopped to stare at a snow laden tree or exclaim over the strange animal on a rock until Andreas showed them is was naught but piled snow. They giggled and chattered the whole way, adding a counterpoint to the crows cawing overhead.

In town the streets crawled with people moving amongst canopied stalls, small braziers lit between to keep the merchants warm. Earlier than usual this year, everyone noticed the descending cold cloak. The inn's cozy interior beckoned with its orange fiery light wavering through the window. Gerta tugged on Andreas's arm. "Let's warm ourselves and have a bite." They ordered mulled cider for the girls and mulled wine for themselves. With some bread and cheese, they nibbled and let their limbs thaw. Gerta smiled happily at Andreas, cheered by the adventure and the murmur of people. "Once we're done, I'll take the girls first so you can drop the blades with the smith. We'll stop at the cloth merchant's to see if there is any wool, and any lovely ribbons."

Her meaningful look told Andreas that should he choose to get some gifts, they would be found there.

"After I take care of the blades, I'll stop at the vintner's and see about having a barrel delivered. I'll meet you at the nut stalls."

They were just bundling the girls up in their coats and mitts when the door opened, admitting a frisson of icy wind that sucked at one's breath. Blocking the doorway was a shadowed figure in furs and wools, lumpy and misshapen.

Gerta gasped and then said, "Oh, good day, Berchta."

Andreas nodded to the woman who seemed buried under the wraps of tattered wolf skin and the wool that encased her. It was as if her head emerged from a bizarre cocoon. She did not frown but seemed to appraise everyone seated within.

To no one person she said, "Do not let this abatement of snowfall lull you. Make sure your homesteads are in order and your hearths cared for. And do not, under any event, go out on Epiphany eve, for ill befalls those who venture abroad." Then she sat, and after a frozen silence, the innkeep brought her a tankard and Andreas and Gerta bustled out the girls, who could do nothing but stare.

Gerta patted her chest as they parted. "Oh that gave me a fright."

Andreas nodded and pulled the blades from the basket. "I expect she'll be around before the advent is complete." He kissed his wife and girls and made his way to the smith's. No one was really comfortable with Berchta. It was hard to strike a conversation with her as it was a fire in rain. Yet at times, when in a well-kept home, she would come out of herself. He shook his head, smiling ruefully. Berchta was odd but she had her kenning in her way and she'd never done them harm no matter what the disgruntled might mutter.

Once the blades were sharpened, and ribbons and other small delights taken care of, Andreas joined his family at the nut stall, helping choose chestnuts, walnuts and almonds. He went back to the inn to gather up their snowshoes. Berchta had moved on but he heard Horst saying, "Young Wilhem took ill and died. And that not a day from when *she* paid her visit. I don't know what she is about but it is no good."

Andreas's anger blistered him. He stood, gripping the snowshoes and glared at Horst. He should say something. What if Horst and the merchants spoke ill of him next? Andreas stomped away, grinding his teeth. Horst had always been pompous. Unfortunately he also could sway the town's council.

Andreas helped the girls into their snowshoes and they left town, the children trailing like ducklings. At the outskirts he ranted about Horst until Gerta called out, "Andreas! Stop. We are not the enemy and we cannot keep up to you in this state."

He stopped and turned, chagrined to see them so far behind, with Gerta encouraging Ingrid who trailed. Striding back to them, he lifted Ingrid. "Hilda, are you okay to continue walking?"

"Yes, Papa," she replied, her green eyes as bright as spring leaves. "You're not mad at me, are you?"

"Oh no, my sweet. No. I am only mad at someone who says bad things about another person."

"But aren't you saying bad things about that man?" She bit at her lip.

Andreas's anger deflated. He sighed. "You are right. I worry because he says bad things that could hurt another person. But you are right. Let us get home."

The clear spell lasted until the beginning of December. Snow fell for days, a steady dusting that made the world scintillate as if scattered with jewels. Hilda looked up one day while building another lopsided snowman, pushing in charred wood for eyes, and said, "Mama, look at the sky. It's sprinkling sugar on us."

After the sugaring of light, dry flakes the land laid muffled, still, holding its breath under the dull gray blanket of clouds. It was during this lull in mid-December, that a dark shape moved toward the farmstead. Andreas noticed it first, having just come from turning the hay in the barn.

"Gerta! Company's coming."

Berchta cleaved the leaden sky from the pale, winter laden earth. As she drew nearer she darkened like a storm. Andreas swallowed but knew there was nothing to fear.

Really, they kept their homestead in order and he didn't believe the tales of her evil eye.

She was swaddled much as she had been in the town over the weeks, her hair writhing over the fur like silvery brown snakes. It was a comfort to know that even she seemed to feel the cold. But how was it then that she walked with an assuredness over deep snow without need of snowshoes? She was of a slight frame to be sure.

"Good day, Berchta." He tipped his head to her.

She nodded in return. "And to you, Andreas. I hope you don't find this an imposition."

"No, my good lady. You are as welcome as always. Gerta has put a kettle on. Would you like to take a look at the barn first? I've just brought the horses in and I'll be bringing the cattle in next."

"I'll help you."

Together they drove the cows back into the barn, Berchta taking a studious but not overly obvious look around. They went to the house, Andreas opening the door for Berchta.

Gerta gave a genuine smile that lit her face, and for which Andreas always loved her. "Berchta, it is good to see you. Come in and warm yourself by the hearth. Can I take your wraps?"

Berchta somehow managed to unwrap the wool layers while leaving the tattered wolfskin still draped upon her shoulders. Her branchlike hands passed the wrap to Gerta, one hand grasping Gerta's plumper one for a moment. "Thank you."

The girls stood wide eyed until Berchta bent over and smiled at them. "And look how well you two have grown from last year. Do you remember me?"

Hilda nodded. "Yes, Berchta, you sometimes give us sweets."

"Hilda!" Gerta exclaimed and Andreas couldn't help but smile. "That's impolite."

Berchta waved her hand. "It is naught but the directness of children."

Andreas lightly touched her shoulder. "Please come sit by the fire for a spell."

Gerta brought over steaming mugs of mulled cider as Berchta told the girls about the flights of snow geese.

Ingrid piped up, "Can I fly too? I'd like to fly."

Bechta's eyes clouded for a moment. "Ah no, little Ingrid, you cannot fly. The soul takes flight at the end of our days and yours is a long way off. Do not pray to fly sooner." She glanced at Hilda too, who looked down silently.

The children seemed a bit cowed but Berchta produced some pink taffy sweets wrapped in waxed parchment. "Here you go, but don't eat them all at once."

They thanked her in unison and scampered off to play.

Berchta looked around appraisingly. "You keep a good home and range. How has your weaving been?"

Gerta smiled, bringing out her spindles. "Andreas makes such lovely spindles for me that they rarely splinter and we can sell some in the town. I've made this linen this year, very soft." She pulled out a folded piece, supple in the candlelight. "A gift for you this advent, Berchta."

Her smiled warmed her stark features. "Thank you for such a lovely present. But remember to keep well your home and do not for any reason venture out this Epiphany eve. There are sights that none should witness and your hearth, home and family are what matter."

Andreas just nodded, looking at his hands. Thus had been her warning each and every year. And all had followed it. There were tales that old Helmut had ventured out one Epiphany eve and that he had been blind from that moment on. No one had ever learned the truth for his mind was addled and his age uncertain.

Berchta stayed a while longer, drinking cider and eating cakes. She commented on the cleanliness of the hearth and the decorative evergreen boughs over the mantle and door.

As she left, Andreas felt the glow of satisfaction. Berchta had seemed pleased.

The weeks leading up to Christmas were bitterly cold, making it difficult to pasture the cattle; everyone relying on the hay and oats they usually laid in for the barren months after Epiphany. Andreas's brief forays into town found Horst and a few others huddled in the inn grumbling over ale rather than tending their homes and fields. Berchta came up often as the cause of their problems.

Each time Andreas left scowling, keeping his mouth closed, but then wondering if he did the right thing. He wasn't afraid of Berchta but was he going to allow the powerful merchants of the town to bully him into silence while they made a fine stew of bile and slanderous words?

It came to a head two days before Christmas day and Andreas's last foray to town for extra feed. He'd spent three days chopping wood and stacking it to dry, preparing for more frigid days. Usually at night they let the fire die to embers, but he had had to pile on a few logs for it was so cold that they woke in the middle of the night and the door was frozen shut in the morning. Gerta had cleaned the ashes from the hearth twice in the last week.

Andreas stopped in at the tavern for ale before he concluded his business, and there were Horst and Bertrand and several other village folk who had had poor crops that year. Horst hunched over his tankard, saying, "I tell you, it is Berchta causing these ills. When that baby eater visits a home, ill befalls it. She probably casts some spell so that the children fail and she collects their flesh. Come spring, it would behoove us to oust her once and for all."

Disgusted, Andreas slammed down his mug, the bench scraping loudly as he stood. The others stared up at him, surprised. "Be that the case, you could blame her for every tragedy that would befall this town for she visits us all. Just as easy to say you or any one is the cause. Look to your own faults before you place them on others." He stormed out, nearly forgetting to pick up the bag of feed before he made for home.

Andreas felt better as he walked. Such men would not compromise his morals. Come death or dishonor, he would choose death and die honorably. He would not forsake those who had done no wrong. No matter what Berchta was, she seemed to straddle the ways between the ancient primal world of animal instincts and turning seasons and the ways of farmers and merchants settled into towns. Andreas would not condemn her on hearsay and he had not seen her hurt anyone.

Andreas glanced at the trees rimed with frost, some looking like hands clawing at the sky. It was said that the old gods walked the land more in winter when mortal folk felt the touch of the wild elements strongest. If they did, Andreas hoped they listened well and knew who brought harm.

Christmas Eve passed in watching the girls opening gifts, of Gerta and Andreas leaning into each other, smiling contentedly. Gerta cooked a wonderful goose on the day of Christmas, everyone pitching in with the chores.

The week that followed was one of deep winter, where Andreas fed the animals: harnesses and shoes, coats and tables were mended and repaired. But Gerta and Andreas stayed close to home through freezing nights. The world seemed dead in its quietness. They played with the girls and enjoyed a short spate through the darkest part of the year.

On the day of Epiphany eve, Andreas crunched over the crust of snow to the barn. As he stocked hay and feed in the barn he checked that the rough hewn doors would hold against any sudden storms. The coop looked fine, the hens softly clucking within. He entered the cottage as the sun slunk behind a white hill, the aroma of spiced apple cider and Yule ale tanged the air. Gerta asked, "You have checked the chickens? Remember, Berchta said to stay inside this night."

Andreas laughed and kissed her worried brow. "Yes, my love, as she always does. No fear. We will be snuggled tight tonight." Gerta had cleaned the hearth, then laid in wood for the evening. He poured the ale and sipped, its warmth spreading. Content, he had another drink at dinner.

Gerta leaned against Andreas, reading a tale of the magi to the girls nestled in their laps. The fire crackled and cast a homely light, its amber glow upon their cheeks. Andreas sipped his ale as the girls began to doze. Gerta finished the tale and softly closed the book. Andreas picked up Hilda as Gerta carried Ingrid. "All right, my sweets, it's time to sleep."

They put them to bed. For a moment they stood close to each other, staring down. Andreas squeezed Gerta's firm bottom and she squeaked, playfully slapping him before they left the room. They kissed before the fire.

"I still have to get the pie filling done for tomorrow," Gerta said as she gently pushed Andreas away. "You amuse yourself for a while."

Andreas sighed dramatically, then smiled, pouring himself another ale before he settled into his chair. He was on another mug by the time Gerta said, "Let's go to bed."

As he stood he lifted her and twirled her around.

"Andreas! Behave," Gerta giggled.

A thump came from out in the yard. Andreas cocked his head and set Gerta down. "I'll be back in a moment. I'm just going to check the barn."

Gerta's eyes grew wide. "No. Remember—"

Trying to hide his slight tipsiness, Andreas said, "Shh, I know. I'm only going a few feet." He slid a finger down her cheek.

Gerta's lips pursed tightly but she said no more as he turned toward the door.

He pulled a stick from the fire and lit the lantern. Pulling on his coat, he stepped into the yard, holding the lantern high. The sky was a black sheet with stars as plentiful as snowflakes, the moon hidden at its dark time. Andreas's breath ringed him like a halo. He teetered into the yard, letting out a subtle burp and laughing.

Tinkling, soft sounds turned into high voices singing and chattering. Andreas stopped and squinted up at the misty shapes. They resolved into children, a tumbling trail behind a figure made of ice and vapor. Andreas's mouthed dropped open. Alighting in his yard was Berchta, now ageless , majestic. Her robes of fur were of the purest white. She swept past him, gliding over the snow, her sleeve brushing him and setting him to shiver at its icy touch.

It was true. Terrified, Andreas could not move, remembering the admonitions, the tales of blinding, the flayer of flesh. But Berchta seemed not to see him as her train of spectral children tottered behind her. There was Wilhelm, who had recently died, lagging behind as he tripped over his nightshirt that wrapped his feet. Every few steps he fell to the earth, trailing farther behind.

Andreas was torn, afraid to be noticed but his heart broke, looking at the little boy. He set the toddler aright and, steadying him with one hand, pulled his garter from his woolen sock. He tied it around the ethereal child's waist and pulled up the nightshirt so it hung above the ground. Tenderly, Andreas smiled at the white-limbed Wilhelm and pushed the boy toward the goddess.

He watched the ghost scamper away and his heart stopped as he looked straight into Berchta's luminescent eyes. She swooped down on the child, her long fingers clutching him up.

Andreas swallowed, frozen in place. Then he heard Hilda's voice.

"Papa? Where are you?" Trailing her blanket, she stood on the cottage's first step.

"Hilda, no!"

Berchta moved to Hilda and all Andreas could do was watch.

But she smiled down upon him, and wrapped Hilda tightly in her blanket. "I guide the innocent souls beyond. They are not responsible for their parent's wrongs."

Little Wilhelm reached for Berchta's hand as she passed Hilda to Andreas. "Your kind hand has always served you well. I take these babes now into my care. My blessings on your own children. They will never want."

Andreas entered the cottage with tears in his eyes.

THE FATHOMLESS WORLD

He had not known of the Covenant for he'd come from a simple place of Maintainers, those who kept others in food, made sure the basics were supplied. But he had always been different. They'd told him his head was in the clouds; that's why he was taller than everyone else. Always placing his imagination upon things and thinking what-ifs, not waiting to see what a thing's story was.

The Tall Man, wrapped in layers of comforting twill, had walked in on the Gawkers concentrating on something in front of them. Short, wild haired, they clustered quietly, layered in plush emerald and cerulean and other rainbow-hued robes. He might have never been noticed, even though he was the only tall man, if he had not pulled his knife and cut a branch from a blue-green barked tree and begun carving it. Now they turned from the golden railing and stared at him instead of at the display, the Forming that had been coalescing before them. The amorphous gas and firmament froze for one moment, then drooped like running wax, speeding up to splash down into the crystal arena, unformed and wasted.

He'd asked what It was going to be, to which they replied, we don't know. You killed it before its Forming. Now one thing has lost its chance at creation.

He broke the Covenant, they said. And he broke the branch. His punishment was swift and resolute. Banished to wander for all time in the Fathomless Building, he was unceremoniously pushed in and the door sealed to blank wall behind him. They'd said there was a small chance, very slim, that he could find his way through his sentence. But he could tell; no one had believed it.

At first he was curious and explored the long corridors, the subtle shades of brown, gray, white and taupe. Every wall met his touch, every corner and pathway he explored, pried at, prodded, pushed. Only the texture of the walls was inconsistent, giving him differentiation. Some revealed rough-hewn brick; others glazed yet monochromatic tiles. There were painted walls and wooden walls and stone walls. Labyrinthine were the corridors, the walls ever changing, corners his only breath of direction.

He wandered for a long time, never hungering, never thirsty, his only company his thoughts. First he ignored those except for the ever present need to escape, to return to the world of flowers and colors and speech. But no passage gave way to his minute examination and later, his frantic clawing.

So he wandered endlessly the corridors of the Fathomless Building. He grew to know his heartbeat well, and the workings of his thoughts, the order they took, the paths they followed. And he began to fathom what was fathomless. One day as he wandered lost in thought, for he could wander the passageways forever, (There was no point to being lost when the configuration changed every day and the halls lead nowhere.) he noticed a very light shadow on a wall. He'd never seen a shadow of any sort in the maze of passages for the light had always been even and inflexible. Even a shadow as fine as a hair, such as this was, attracted his attention and curiosity. As he gazed at it, pondering the reality of it, the colors it imparted to the wall, the means and juxtaposition of a line on a plane, he became aware that it stretched to the floor.

The Tall Man had never lost faith for he had never really had it; not in a way in which he could say, I believe. But he had never despaired. He had feared, been bored and become resigned to his fate, but he had never given up. Now his surprise slowly awoke him from his somnambulant, introspective state. As the realization dawned in him a flush of warmth flared outward from his heart, heating his face and feet and hands, adding a touch of rose to skin that had taken on the monotonous hues of the Fathomless Building.

His long wanderings had brought him a change of view and a change of heart, a remorse for his ignorance, his loss and his careless arrogance. He longed for sound where here even his words had been swallowed by the muffling silence. As he reached out and tentatively, unbelievingly touched the dark line it deepened and spread, moving at right angles to form a door. A door that matched the wall except for that thin seam of shadow. His heart raced now, believing before his mind did that here was hope, a change at long long last.

There was no knob or handle, no hinge. It could be a trick, perhaps another passageway being born before his eyes. But he could not resist a new sensation. He placed first his long fingers upon the wall and then laid his palm flat against it. Slowly, hesitantly he pushed. The right side swung out and he thought surely his heart would stop after so long a restless wandering.

As the door swung open a light brighter and harder than what had filled the Building shone in, almost turning his skin translucent. He squinted against the harshness and felt a refreshing, cold blast of air. Breathing in, he stepped through the door, into a world of white upon white.

Where the Fathomless Building had always displayed a corner or a wall ahead, here there was only a vast flat horizon. Above, lay the frigid ether of white sky and where it met the earth was barely discernible. The ground spread out, an infinite ivory blanket of snow. His breath puffed out in colorless vapor as he stared incredulously. Slowly, he turned a circle and except for the Fathomless Building, now as sealed tightly against him as it had once held him in, there was nothing but white. Snow and ice and cold.

The austere, glacial beauty, as much as the freezing wasteland, left him breathless. He turned and stared, squinting against the bleaching light, trying to see if anything marred the horizon. Eyes so used to a monochrome of browns and beiges saw instantly the subtle shades and contours of pale green and blue that marked ice and snow.

The Tall Man first walked around the Fathomless Building. From the outside its façade was bleaker than had been its interior. There were no doors, no windows, and it was flat on top so no pinnacle of roof could be seen. It looked to be three maybe four stories tall but looks could be deceiving on something with no detail. Done looking at the Building he circled again, going in the other direction and surveyed the land in all directions. Small humps and dips showed the landscape was not perfectly flat but it had little in the way of features. The only way to keep any sense of bearings would be to keep the Fathomless Building in sight.

Rubbing his chilly hands together, blowing on them with slow breath, the Tall Man picked a direction, but how does one tell a direction from another when they all look the same? So he dug in his pockets and found the old bluish branch he had once started to carve; the beginning of his destiny. He carefully placed it upon the ground in front of one side and began walking. The squeak and crunch of snow beneath his feet accompanied him. He walked, and walked and walked, turning ever so often to see if the Building still maintained its vigil.

He walked for a very long time and the light never wavered nor changed. It was as if he was in the Fathomless World now. He stooped and scooped up a handful of snow, packing it into a ball. Then he threw it as far as he could but he could not see it land for it blended into the background, its individuality being absorbed back to nothing. Sighing, he walked on. When next he looked back, the Building had dwindled to size of his pinky nail. Still, he trudged on, the cold permeating him to his core so that he felt as if he too were ice. And perhaps, he mused, he was for his feelings, his emotions had subsided as he had wandered through the years. They were as bland as the limited colors he had moved through.

Eventually, for there was no way of discerning time that was also absent in this place, he turned and saw the building was no bigger than a pinprick of taupe on the horizon. Any farther and he would lose it, and yet, there was nothing to show any change but the space of that building's occupation. He returned along the same path he had taken but he could not see his footprints for they had been obliterated by the lack of defining light.

When he reached the building, he kept the wall to his right and walked to the opposite side. Rooting about in his pockets yielded a loose thread that he plucked and laid upon the crust of wintry ground. Luckily the thread was gray for had it been white it would have been swallowed by the overwhelming blankness. Again he walked until the Building was no more than a dust mote and again he returned.

He now went to one of the other sides, no longer even knowing from which wall he had been birthed into this soulless world. Taking the last possession from his pocket, his knife, he sawed through the threads of one of his coat buttons, and placed the pale blue shell button upon the ground. When he had completed yet another interminably long walk into nothingness and returned he went to the last side and pulled out his knife. In comparison to the land about him its steel seemed to positively shine like a star. He stabbed it into the ground where it melted a small crack but his body temperature had lowered to the point where he was not much but a frosty apparition upon the surface.

The Tall Man completed his last long walk, even moving beyond the view of the Fathomless Building, which now seemed fathomable in retrospect. He did not waver but still everything remained the same and so, in resignation of his new punishment he returned.

When he reached the wall he pulled his knife out and slid down to sit upon the unforgiving snow. He twirled the knife, looking down at its shiny surface. Something as simple as a sunbeam seemed so far away. He longed for a blade of grass, a beetle, a child's laughter. He longed until he thought his heart would crack but it too now held a layer of hoarfrost. Closing his eyes, he tried to will himself to sleep, to hibernation but as hunger and thirst had deserted him, so had sleep. Suicide was still a fleeting specter for though he was stuck in an eternity of nothing, he was not yet ready to be part of it, even though he already was in a sense.

Someday, some indefinable date in his future, he knew there might be a time when he would welcome the ending of his breath and heart, a silencing of his thoughts and roaming. But not yet.

It was then that the thought struck as if his blade had turned upon him, stabbing him to the quick. No others had made it through the punishment. They had slowly been absorbed back into the primordial void, where absence of all had finally sapped them of their selves. The Tall Man shuddered violently and stood.

This would not happen to him. His crime had been ignorance but that was no reason to be obliterated, gone from memory in all senses. He tightly gripped his knife in his gaunt white hands and walked a ways from the building. Chewing his cheek, squinting in all directions, he finally chose a small hump of palest jadeite ice. Squatting down, he hacked with ferocity until he had a chunk about three times the size of his head. Sitting upon the hard ground, he pulled the ice to him and began to carve at it, muttering.

His hands quickly grew numb but he did not care. He would not let the rest of him join the numbness. Delicately, with complete concentration for nothing existed to distract him, he chiseled and dug until a shape took form. Slowly a giant pallid rose in bloom appeared.

Dropping the knife beside the ice bloom, he now rolled snow into a ball, and then more snow into a larger ball, and last the largest ball. Piling the medium snowball onto the large one, he then placed the last on top, forming a featureless snowman. Digging out more ice, he made eyes, nose and mouth, all of the same creamy whiteness.

The challenge grew in him and he carved long blocks of ice and snow. Some were square, some oblong, others trapezoidal. Soon, in a relative space of timelessness, the landscape was littered with obelisks and dolmens. The Tall Man worked tirelessly.

He carved beautiful dancers precariously balanced en point. He sculpted animals from his imagination, from the dreams of his waking mind. He peopled the landscape with figures; children, men, women, behemoths and minutiae of vermin. As he worked he talked to them, giving them names. Madness had come to him but he did not care. He would talk and form this featureless wasteland into something.

Great winged birds swooped down on minuscule stalagmites. The tiniest creatures flew around minarets, the barest point of each wing adhering to the greater ice column. Trees and flowers, frosty and crystalline took form, creating a forest. He worked on and on, filling the land on all sides of the Fathomless Building. It there had been the tiniest beam of sunlight the statues would have glittered like a palace of gems. Instead, they stood mute; great cats, leaf hoppers, fish joined head to tail, furniture, books, scrolls, lamps, serpents, leviathans of the seas, whimsical wish granters, great rock dwellers, a menagerie of thousands upon thousands of things, many lifetimes of sculpting.

The Tall Man's knife wore down. Still he carved and talked to his creations but one unending day he stopped. He stopped carving, he stopped talking. He stopped and dropped the knife and looked around. Stumbling backward to the Building, he surveyed his handiwork but what he saw was infinity. Infinite madness. His back hit the wall and he slid down, crumbling into a heap upon the now well-packed ice. Something cracked, broke and fell asunder. A tear, crystal clear, pooled in the corner of his eye and rolled over the lid, hesitantly sliding down his cheek, the first of its kind until it leapt from the ledge of his chin to the snowy ground below. As it fell, it slid into a small crack first formed so long ago by the Tall Man wedging his knife in the snow. Down fell that drop, down and down into the minute crevice, dropping down its heat beneath the surface.

The Tall Man did not notice as his tears, now braver after the first fellow's sacrifice, rolled freely from his eyes. They began their slow venturing and soon an army followed as he crumpled completely upon the ground. Curled tight around his broken mind and heart he howled despair and loneliness and madness. Worst of all he wept his utter defeat, his abandonment and howled. He wailed as unceasingly as he had worked, crying his heart out.

As his heart bled out through his eyes, clear and pure, it let out all that he was. There was no hate, no greed, no envy. There was only surrender and loneliness following on the long lost heels of compassion and curiosity. He did not notice in his all-consuming grief (a fitting stage in a place that had been all consuming) that his tears puddled about him, melted some of the ice and snow and formed small pools.

As the salty tears spread they touched the base of the rose, his first statue, and a tentative blush of pink moved through its petals. Next, a great fish tail met the salt waters. The tail rippled, starting to flip as the fish's silvery sides took on hue. Its eyes rolling, its mouth gaping, it made for the ever widening pool of tears. A waterfall shimmered to life, falling blue and frothy into a great basin turning the color of pale gray marble.

Fairies flying around a minaret turning orange and blue and green shuddered minutely, then broke free of the base's clasp and fluttered to the forest. A tree rooted in brown and vermillion and peridot shot up its branches, rustling them with emerald life. Everywhere a cacophony of light and sound unfolded. A rainbow and more of color burst over the landscape, spreading like a sunrise: carnelian, verdigris, charcoal, azure, aquamarine, amethyst, lilac, ruby, magenta. Everything was touched; even what remained white took on hue and shade and shadow.

The Tall Man hiccupped, pulling in a shuddering breath. His madness was firming in him now. He opened his eyes on his surrender.

THE FISHWIFE

When first they were wedded and he was pulled to the ships, she paced the tide in and out, in and out, in and out, watching always for that first sail, but only seeing the sea. Every beachcombed button, or sharp eye of glass, or water-loved timber she questioned and held and listened. Like tide, she could not leave, could not stay and dreaded, yet hoped for a sign. When the first shy finger of sail appeared she would hasten up the beach, her footprints following behind. A flurry of dusting, cleaning and freshening, then a pinch to her cheeks for love. But it was never needed for her heart would pound the shore and she'd be waiting and roping her hands in her apron.

It's been more than ten knots and nearly as many years and the long long days of gutting fish alone are enough to make her yearn for the sea. She's seen more fish than grains of sand. Their glistening cold bodies and dead eyes like the moon captured and demeaned, jellylike things, leave her wanting nothing but turnips or lettuce and peas. Her heart has paled like those fisheyes, but always the good wife she carts the fish to market.

Prow-straight, her back propels her to town, with a "Good day to you and to you." Her stall is clean and her fish don't speak of days left in the sun. She greets all, like the cries of gulls but more of a wren's song. The mongers would love to hate her, circle in talk and look for the tarnish when they say she carries herself like a lady. How'd she come to be only a fishwife, with a husband always merchanting the sea? Surely she fell from some better station.

They can dig in, but she's like grains of sand on a beach, and they can't lessen her status. She gives, she moves, yet she's always the same.

The town is a whole. Without her they'd lessen, yet they want her and wish she was gone. No gossip from her, her head held proud and her seashell complexion so smooth. Without her they think they'd shine brighter. No one looks deeply, nor would if they could. Her faults could reflect their own flaws.

She feels herself erode, buffeted by wind and bird cries and sea spray. Where is the ship that will let her adventure, feel the safe passage away from the swirling undertow? Waves, wind and an errant husband fill her with a need to seek. But what? She yearns, but can't pull herself from beneath the heavy flipping bodies of fish. Their entrails, a red and bruised blue tangle, pull her feet down in their bloody moorings.

Not all the men who surge through the town admire her masthead stance. One cobbler, one smith, and one fisherman do dream to catch her on their hooks. The eyes of the smith, cobbler and fisherman, when she glances up from a sale, look like the moon too, captured and small. But there's the banker, who rustles as he walks, who has stock on her soul.

The day is done soon with all the fish schooled in paper and sent to warm waiting pans. Like lovers, she wraps the last two away and cradles them in her basket. Like falling shells, chatter fills the air. Everyone, now friendly, can taste the flavor of home. Small talk to hasten the hour on its way. "Ever seen the silks and spices they brought from Sumatra last year? Pirates, you think?"

A smile flies over her face, shakes her head. Not this coast. The shore, too rocky.

No worry, really, with her husband just gone for a month this time and not so many salty dogs to bark at the heels of marauders. The town holds little and the fishwife knows her cottage is safe.

Way—aaaay up she rises, her skirt billowing behind. She begins her walk, with haste, a wave good-bye and an eye to the sky for rain. The clouds tumble, restless, hiding their blue treasure.

Two stops before home. Two stops and the difference between pearl and swine. The first house, grand, serene atop a low hill. Clean glass presents its face to the first slashes of rain. A separated lover, the fishwife leaves one fish in the basket, the other, entwined in her arms. At the door, a light rap, and heartbeats, only two pass.

The door shyly reveals the man who beckons her into soft luminescence, away from the furious rain. The wind peers up her dress as he closes the door. She offers the fish on two outstretched arms, a quiver that could be the chill. "A fish," she says, "a nice fresh fish. Only a day old if it's that."

He smiles and takes the fish from her arms. His watch fob winks, telling her that he knows the time. "I'll get several good meals from that. Cook will be pleased." His hand closes on hers; warmth seeps into her chilled limbs.

"Come, sit, and warm yourself. I'll bring you some tea. It's cook's night off." The banker bleeds off into shadows, warm aromas of bread. And she, still, waiting.

Wind beats at the door, tries to whisper her back to its side. The shell of the house hugs her, leaves her dreaming on the sofa, red-faced, plush as a vixen, and deep curtains wall out the world.

Cool porcelain, then warmth slides into her hands. She gives his gaze a small smile. Within, the tide is pulling; she is afraid of being drawn out. A sip, warm slides into her belly, waves move out faster and faster.

He takes the cup, sets it on the table and kisses her hands then her arm. "So much," he says, "so much time since I've seen you." He's missed her and wants her, he breathes. The warm flesh of his lips find her cheek. Then the pink anemone of his tongue flicks into her mouth, roams the ridge of her teeth.

A small rat is chewing at the fiber of her will. She is fraying, coming apart, opening.

The pounding surf echoes her heartbeats as he lays his head upon her breast. His fingers undo her buttons and clasps, loosen the stays that have bound her. Her clothes cascade away from his touch till she lays, white pearl of her skin in his embrace.

His tongue circumnavigates her body, rings her coral nipple. She sighs, knowing that it has all led to this, the weeks and visits before. No obvious increase in attention but the banker's interest unflagging.

It is not for love or for lack of love that she does this. A sailor could not propel her forward, yet the banker's rich trappings might net her the new. She hopes he can release the storm that beats galeforce against her. She rides the waves of her reputation and his. No one knows, would expect this fishwife and a stalwart banker to couple in a seaweed tangle of clothes.

It's over but she feels the crashing inside, not yet tamed, the rage of waves. She puts herself back together, cleans up, wrapped in the sheaf of her respectable world. He grasps her hand, presses in coin for the food. A nice catch, he smiles, sure that the pirate's horde of silver is his.

The rain falls steadily, resolutely as she picks her basket up from the side of the house and leaves, no backward good-byes. One more stop, the missing unearthed perhaps, then she'll set out for home.

The other place is a long way from town, the bare plain shack of a home, kept up well but lacking all niceties. The rocky shore looms close here; waves reach up and over, trying to find purchase on land. Her rap is louder, bolder to outshout the storm's own chorus.

The door opens and a strong dark hand pulls her in quickly, slams the door shut before the wind catches its breath. He takes her proffered fish, drops coin in her hand, then stares at her in the gold light of candles lit like many fever bright eyes.

No pleasant talk, no misleading cheer or camouflage tea, she is upon him, her lips seeking blindly, searching a way to his own inner lure. He falls back from her, tugs her with him, tumbles into the parlor, onto his knees.

Her hands crab over his heart, scuttle the shirt away from his dark matted chest. She gasps, churns her hips as she gives all to the flesh. Up she rises, up goes the skirt of her dress, the damp white lace of petticoats. Always she feeds on his hot hard lips, tongue probing for lusty wet treasure. His callused fingers squeeze the meat of her buttocks, bring her forward as her hands reach down, deep down and release him.

Who's tethered, who's not? Who's captured and released? She plays him out then draws him in. Does he crawl from the shore into her dark churning depths? Does she fight or leap from his lead?

Her hair loosens from frenzy, unleashed. Sweat rains down on his face. The waves, the swell have pulled her in. What am I? she cries into the cavern, echoing within. What makes me different? If there are answers, they're lost in the roar.

Long ago the waves pulled her apart and showed her lust has little to do with love. The fishwife searched and found the edge of a discovered land, her place beside her husband. But more she wanted, more within, an undiscovered sea. Love's tenuous anchoring on her heart and body crumbled away with her even keel. Bearings lost, she could no more tell if she was fishwife, woman, shore, waves or the ship of his desires. She circled herself, at once crying gull and waves.

Heave ho, she's up and straightening her clothes, casting a distant smile to her carpenter. Her fingers walk the coastline of his jaw, then she turns, admits herself to the wind.

Ho, what treasure does she store in her holds, this ship adrift? The white spume of two or three good men. A treasure ship, if the rats and salt water don't get to it first.

Her cottage, near, meekly eyes the beach where hungry rivulets crawl toward the door. Her basket, dropped, accepts her clothes. Rain and wind dance on her flesh and she rubs in sand and brine. Faint lanterns, her eyes, shine on the waves before she blinks out rain and runs to the door.

Inside, she is tossed to the land of dreams. Restless, rolling, hands snake through the bedsheets. Dawn, still submerged, and night's beginning to drown when she wakes to the absence of sound. No fighting waves or moaning wind or manic tap-dancing rain. Silence.

The sailor's wife still feels the storm, churning green. The door yawns hugely as she emerges into the dawn gray. The ocean, calm as an upturned pewter plate. Balling her gown up against her belly, her chest, she tries to stand astride the calm she beholds.

Lids shutter on her eyes, then open. A small beacon shines brightly in the dark lands of her mind. It is the water, the ocean whose tide draws all out. She feels she is but is not water, will not return as tide and rain and streams. She is not the shore or rocky outcrops luring ships to their deaths, or standing against the beat of time. She is not the ship or sea that can carry dreams, that seeks unthinkingly and returns. She is only a wife, a fishwife.

Gown puddles at her feet as she steps free. Her husband can't bring her life wrapped in silk. The banker can't lure her with gold. Her carpenter lover, so daring and rough, cannot build for her a house of life. Seek, and be, she walks to the shore, lets the water lick her toes, lap her knees, caress her thighs.

She swims, sleek and silvery. Pulled on by the fish she has married, she dives out of sight.

SHOES

It was a nightmare, finding the shoes. Albeit dusty, the ruby sparkle still showed through, after all those years. She'd been so young and trusting then, but an involuntary trip to a land with flying monkeys, attack crows and sinister trees makes anyone grow up quickly.

Dorothy reached into the back of the closet and pulled out the leather, jewel-encrusted shoes. In their gaudiness they were shoes only a child could love; a trap any child would fall for. They had been silver once, when on the feet of the dead witch and Dorothy's own, but the witch's blood had soaked into them, adding a touch of her hidden charms, and after the field of poppies they'd bloomed crimson. Childhood had been abandoned like a lost doll at that point.

Shivering, Dorothy shied away from the memories and what she couldn't remember. The poppies had brought a languid sleep, a sea of red that bled into her vision. They, her companions, had carried her, they said, but what else had been done to turn the shoes scarlet? Kneeling in front of the closet of faded, well-worn clothes, Dorothy let her hands brush over the shoes, removing layers of grime and lost years that danced as fairy motes in the late afternoon light. It should have been a comfort, knowing that she hadn't made it up, that enduring the taunts of "Dotty Dot" had been worth it. There should have been solace for all she had borne, but like the Lost Boys, she only felt unsettled.

Dorothy stared at the shoes daily, wondering what they were trying to tell her. Keeping up the farm allowed her little time to idle over the past. But events happened to remind her.

There was the day she drove the tractor out into the field and a murder of crows took flight, blistering the sky. Their silence shuddered her ears and she stopped, peering into the black mass. Crows weren't unusual but that they had remained silent was. Could these crows have known of the murder in Oz, the witch only a wisp of memory? Were they plotting against her? Why now? Had the shoes eventually pointed the way?

She shook her head, her braids flopping against her shoulders. That was nonsense. If you looked for coincidence, you'll find coincidence. But she carried her rifle after that, just in case.

Like the birds, her memories wheeled around to her return from that land. So sure had she been of Oz's existence that she had insisted in telling her story. Aunt Em and Uncle Henry had been relieved to have her back at first, having assumed that she'd been killed in the cyclone, but their belief had faded with her wild tales. They'd convinced themselves and her that she'd been swept up and suffered amnesia, been delusional, had a knock on the head, something that left her wandering aimlessly for months. That explained the different clothes. It didn't explain why, two months later, Dorothy, after suffering knife stabbing cramps, released a small bloody mass into the toilet.

She had told no one, not wanting to end up in some sanitarium. That scarlet letter would never spell a word. And *that*, she had had no story for. One day, she had then vowed, she would leave Kansas for good, with its pressing heat, and sinister winds that could smother a life forever.

One day…

Every day Dorothy went to the closet and looked at the shoes. Sometimes she pulled them out and just stared at them. She didn't think of trying them on, not really.

Inevitably, she would toss the insidious footwear back and go about the day's work.

Increasingly, she would stop in the middle of milking a cow, of herding the cattle, of using the tractor to cut the golden hay, and just daydream. What-ifs buzzed about her as thickly as the wicked witch's black bees. But dreams too fell dead at her feet like those expired insects.

It hadn't been pleasant but it had been memorable. An adventure. That world had little in common with this farm, and Dorothy could have walked from fencepost to teetering fencepost blind, she knew it so well. But it was more that the land had been ground down, buffeted by rain, tornados and snow, until its image had been branded into her skin. Gritty and no nonsense.

There had been plenty of nonsense in Oz. It was founded on the incomprehensible. Still, for Oz, the Scarecrow had been remarkable in his way, animated, searching for thoughts when they filled his straw-stuffed head already.

And the Tin Woodman who had endured such terrible torture, being cut limb from limb; a will to live so strong it could not rust. Now *that* had been heart. Even the Lion, in a place where all the animals talked, managed some compassion. Those creatures, not one of them really human, had all gone on to rule. But Dorothy had really only been herself, a hero by chance and a slave by ignorance. She had been a child wanting the comfort of home, be it ever so dreary. There had never been a grand plan, or ambition for something larger. The dry Kansas dirt that swirled in under the doors had permeated slowly, making it impossible to see the future when keeping it at bay took part of every day.

Before she knew it, Henry and Em's life had become hers. Dorothy supposed she should be grateful. Just as in Oz she'd been given a means to return home. But she'd never asked for any of it, except for going home. She had never had a grand plan like the Wizard.

A week later Dorothy walked the fence line, checking that the boards held firm. A couple of cows had been found wandering in the neighboring field. She'd stumbled over something in the grass, crunching metallically under her foot. A collection of old tin cans shot through, pitted and rusted to the color of dried blood, rested in the tufted grass by a fencepost. People always took potshots and practiced in the fields, but why did these ones lie in the figure of a man, a small metal funnel touching like a cap? She kicked at them to find that dirty string held them together. It tangled about her foot, the tins rising up until she had beaten them flat with the butt of her rifle. Then they had fallen lifeless to the earth as Dorothy wiped the sweat from her eyes.

Down to earth. That's what they had always told her. "Dorothy you gotta come down to earth." "You need to be more down to earth. " She had stopped talking of Oz, stopped imagining a better future. A different place. So down to earth had she become that she was an extension of the land. It was as if she had become one of those defensive trees that had snared the Scarecrow until the Tin Man lopped off the offending limbs. Rooted, she could only wave her arms about, evict crows and trespassers with a strong word and the motion of a rifle, if need be. But she was as planted as ever any tree had been.

Ten years had spun away. First Aunt Em died of a cough that wouldn't quit, and two years later, Uncle Henry (who had never been able to remove the gray with which Kansas had painted him) up and expired of hard living. Dorothy had worked the farm alone for the past seven years and felt much older than her twenty-five.

She had pulled the shoes out again and absentmindedly rubbed them as she thought of Aunt Em and Uncle Henry. After Aunt Em's and Uncle Henry's deaths, Dorothy had been less likely to go to town. Sure, she needed supplies but socializing always made her feel more alone. She had never had close friends after Oz. Toto had been a loving little companion. He'd never been that bright, even for a dog but his antics had made her laugh. She'd thought of getting another dog or several but she still missed Toto's happy-go-lucky ways.

The dust from the shoes now stuck to her fingers, making them gray. She rubbed her fingers together thoughtfully. The gray had once been everywhere. Now the fields were green like the Emerald City but the gray still trickled down within the chinks, mortaring her to a family tradition. Tossing the shoes back into the closet, she stood and wiped her hands on her jeans, then turned to stare out the window at the fields of corn.

Oz had been no delusion, no fevered imagining. The shoes had led her through a change of perspective, and they had led her out. Trying to banish the uncomfortable memories, she grabbed up the broom and swept the porch, shooing the chickens away. But she was caught up in the colors of the fields. Of all the colors of Oz, the meek blue Munchkins, the timid yellow Winkies, the grandiose Emerald City and the green-haired girl, it was the red that still shaded her vision. The poppy fields, the shoes, the red-uniformed girls and the russet tones of Glinda's hair. The witch has been so kind, giving Dorothy a kiss full of succulent regret, or places yet to explore, and the secret for leaving.

Grabbing a beer, Dorothy opened the screen door to the porch, letting it squeak and softly bang shut. She sat in a creaky wooden chair that Uncle Henry had made. Like that sturdy piece of furniture, Dorothy had grown up plain. If she'd remained a beauty, not even the stigma of being crazy would have kept the boys away. "No nonsense" is what Aunt Em would have called it. Dorothy was no nonsense. No gingham pinafores or white silk gowns now. They just wouldn't do on a farm. And no ruby slippers for skipping through surreal landscapes.

"It all became no nonsense after that, didn't it, Toto?" Then she remembered again that he had died the year before. She sighed and sipped the beer. "No nonsense."

It began to bother Dorothy, thinking of Oz, the shoes, Toto and all those odd inhabitants of a decade gone. Of course she had had no responsibilities, protected by her companions. She'd done nothing by design, not even killing the witch. A fortuitous accident, some had called it. It hadn't been a pleasant journey but Dorothy had been alive. So what was life? Was there really so little to do on the farm that she could ponder the past?

In truth, what she did exhausted the body but rarely the mind. It would have been likely for a little girl to fabricate a world seeking relief from boredom. Except for the shoes. Why had they returned after so long? Why beckon forth those images now? After she had had to endure the comments, looks and ridicule of her town. After she'd lost all hope of a different world. Could someone have sent them, because they needed her, wanted her in Oz? Were they hunting her?

By rights she should throw the shoes away, but she was afraid to cut off that avenue of escape. Oz might only be a few steps away. So Dorothy continued to regard them, hold them and finally, once even try them on (miraculously they still fit her feet).

She chewed her lip and paced at night, a beer in her hand. Walking the fields under a harvest moon, listening to the crickets, she searched for the love she had felt here. The fields may have been green but all had turned to dust: in the end it was the dust and gray that claimed Aunt Em and Uncle Henry. She did love the sunset and the smell of cut hay, the musky barn scent of the cows, but there was a grittiness to everything.

Dorothy stopped in the field, staring up at the stars sprinkled like daisies in the meadow of night. She had loved "here." And she had loved in Oz. Her unlikely companions had been friends and family but she had never been kissed by a man. Not there. Not here. It was the Witch of the North, mysterious and never named, who had kissed her upon arriving; and the Witch of the South, Glinda who kissed her upon leaving. Her journey had begun and ended with a kiss, but she had never thought what she really wanted.

In Kansas everyone is aware of the weather if they don't want to become victim of it. Sometimes it was lightning storms and sometimes it was strong winds debating if they would work themselves into a frenzy. That night Dorothy closed the storm shutters, made sure the cattle were safe in the barn and kept a flashlight by the bed, and the trap door accessible in the next room.

Normally the howling wind alerted her to a tornado. That night she slept well until a horrendous banging and scraping bolted her awake. She could hear the wind but no more than that. Yet something…someone?...banged at the door.

Heart beating so loudly that she could barely hear, Dorothy took deep breaths to calm herself and grabbed the rifle. In pajamas and bare feet, she quietly moved toward the door. When the front window was in sight, she saw through the muslin curtains that a shutter had come loose and the shadow of something, someone was at her door. What was he doing? What did he want? She shouted, "Get away from the door or I'll blow a hole in you!"

The banging continued.

"What do you want?"

No answer. And then the wind let up and the shadow was gone. Dorothy waited a few minutes, letting her adrenalin settle, then cautiously approached the door. She peeked out but could see nothing. Rifle at the ready, she threw open the door and looked around. The wind shrieked and a man threw himself on her. Screaming she beat him back and shot without thinking.

Shaking, she looked down and saw a figure on the ground. Her rifle held ready, she took a step closer and prodded him. He was soft…too soft. Then, she realized it was a scarecrow blown loose by the wind. But it had been at her door, wanting to come in.

She shuddered and ran back into the house, locking the door. Making strong coffee, she wrapped herself in a blanket and sat on the couch for the rest of the night. Oz wanted her. What would come next? A lion, a pack of wolves, the hideous yet noble flying monkeys? Her past was trying to reclaim her. It would be like before: she would be pulled along, red shoes and all, with hollow kisses to set her on the road. Would she ever get to make her own choices?

Just before dawn when the sky had moved from black to the deepest teal, Dorothy crawled into bed and slept.

When she awoke, she fed the chickens and the cows. Then she made a few calls. Back in her room, she pulled out a large green backpack, still looking as if it had never been used. There would be no baskets this time. Carefully going through her wardrobe, she chose the most colorful shirts, some jeans and cutoffs, a good pair of sport shoes, her western boots, and, after a moment's hesitation, the ruby slippers.

She packed the clothes, leaving the footwear out for now, then went to her safe and took her bank card and the savings. When all that was done she walked slowly to the bathroom. Staring into the mirror, she undid her auburn braids, which brought her hair to just past mid back. She cocked her head from side to side, then picked up the scissors. Carefully, with comb in hand, she cut her hair to just above her shoulder. The past was the past. Then she had a good long shower, scrubbing the night's scare from her skin.

After she was dressed, she went through the kitchen and chose sausage, cheese, crackers, a few tins of tuna and granola to put in the pack. Finally, done, she surveyed her place, a half smile touching her lips. Dorothy made one last call. "Hi. Yeah, I'm ready to go. I appreciate you looking after the place. No, I'm not sure how long I'll be gone. Use what you can, whatever you like. The key is under the watering can. Bye. Thanks."

Dorothy stood still for a moment, eyes closed, feeling the vibrations around her, breathing deep the fresh scent of hay, the tired dusty smell of wood. Listening to the distant call of swallows, the contented lowing of the cows, she knew it all was a part of her; Oz and Kansas, but it was the past. It was a moment of change and she wanted to remember it well.

Back in the bedroom, she rummaged around until she found one of Aunt Em's old lipsticks. It was somewhat dry but there was enough to it to put some color onto her lips. Ruby red. She smiled, pocketed the lipstick, and then turned to pack the footwear into her pack.

Lifting it, she was happy to find it wasn't too heavy. Dorothy grabbed the keys to her old car and left the house, locking the door.

She took one look at the scarecrow and turned her back on it, moving to the watering can.

Dorothy stopped again, looking at the keys. Glinda had awakened her in many ways. She turned back to the house and rummaged in her pack. Pulling out those crimson shoes, she ran her fingers over their sharp texture one more time, sniffed the muskiness of old leather and placed them on the porch near the scarecrow. Just as she had had the magic of the shoes all the time she was in Oz, she realized she had always had the secret for leaving. Her last adventure had begun with the shoes and a kiss.

Dorothy blew a kiss to the house and fields. This time she would do it on her own.

AFTERWORD

When I was younger I used to walk up the alley to an empty lot. We lived at the edge of the city in Calgary, Alberta, near Spy Hill. This undeveloped house lot was a safe haven from a chaotic family life. I would lie amongst the dandelions and bluebells and stare at the night sky, filled with stars, a carpet encrusted with shining possibilities. I contemplated life, the cosmos and what lay hidden in all that vast space. I hoped to see a UFO, or have some emissary from beyond descend and whisk me off to a better life. And sometimes those possibilities scared me.

We live in worlds of what-if all the time. Some are the mundane; what if I'm late for work, what if I bought these shoes, what if I took a vacation in Europe, what if I leave my partner? Sometimes we live the what-ifs of the past. I should have bought that house, I shouldn't have said that terrible thing. We speculate and wonder and it makes the world a richer place and indeed gives us worlds to explore.

My childhood, like many people's, was not a happy time. In fact, as is often the case, we forget the mundane of every day, the joys fade to pale reminiscence, and we remember the dark moments. There was no escape from childhood, except through books. I had always been attracted to art, and remember drawing a picture of a pansy in a vase when I was six. My mother praised it and it might have been that praise alone that made me want to be an artist. So I drew and even painted when later my mother paid for private painting lessons. I even went to the Alberta College of Art and Design after high school.

While the visual arts had always been part of my youth, I had started writing as an escape at about the age of twelve. My first writing was poetry but I began a novel in junior high school of which I wrote fifty pages. I still have this early, unfinished piece, and it pretty much sucks. The story was reminiscent of Ray Bradbury's stories and of *The Most Dangerous Game,* both of which had left a strong impression.

Every tale is a genesis of sorts, whether that of the character, the world in which the story takes place, or the writer's process. One of my earliest stories was from a dinosaur's point of view as the meteor struck Earth. Another was of a person with powers but not enough that they could help anyone. Even then the dark element was present, even if those stories are now lost. But then the dark side, the shadow, whether you label it horror, fantasy, thriller or frisson is really just conflict. And for many, the greatest conflict is with time.

I explore these dark veins as a way of controlling my own darkness. We are all made of light and dark. What trials does a person face? Does nature or humankind triumph? True horror means a person resists, fights, perseveres but does not prevail. The "other" is too powerful. H.P. Lovecraft's Cthulhu mythos dealt with the horror of the other and the great insignificance of a mere mortal. Any heroic fantasy from Tolkien's *Lord of the Rings* to Rowlings' Harry Potter books delves into fighting the other but triumphing over evil. They are about hope and perseverance.

The tales here are about dark desires and deadly choices. They are all stories of personal trials and tribulations, where sometimes the character is tempted and often he or she is transformed. A fellow writer once asked me what theme I explored and I didn't know. Yet, in compiling this mostly reprint collection I can now say that I write morality tales, situations and events that challenge the character's very essence. Not every story is about facing or overturning morals but the majority do challenge the protagonist's (or antagonist's) beliefs and values.

Fiction does not always entertain; it can generate conversation or discomfort. It can inspire new creations and bring about wonder. While this collection begins with the darker tales of downfall and horror, I end the book on a lighter note, where hope may be evident on the road into the future. Amongst the embers of the fallen, there is a spark that will come to life and bring new journeys.

—Colleen Anderson

CREDITS

An Ember Amongst the Fallen
—first published in *Evolve: Vampire Stories of the New Undead,*
Edge Science Fiction and Fantasy Publishing, 2010
Consuming Fear
—first published *Northern Frights 4,* Mosaic Press, 1997
Amuse-Bouche
—first published *Shroud Magazine #2,* 2008
What Strange Fruit
—previously unpublished
It's Only Words
—first published *The Horror Anthology of Horror Anthologies,*
Nemonymous Press, 2011
Exegesis of the Insecta Apocrypha
—first published *Horror Library Vol. 4,* Cutting Block Press,
2010, honorable mention: *The Year's Best Fantasy &*
Horror
On Wings of Angels
—first published *Vestal Review #7,* 2001
Phoenix Sunset
—first published *Tesseracts 3,* Press Porcepic, 1990, &Twilight
Tales website 2000
Lover's Triangle
— first published *On Spec,* 1996, *Dreams of Decadence,* 2001,
New Vampire Tales, Books of the Dead Press, 2010
Ice Queen
—first published *Warrior Wisewoman,* Norilana Books, 2008

Hold Back the Night
—first published *Open Space,* Red Deer Press, 2003,
        shortlisted for the Gaylactic Spectrum award & the
        Speculative Literature Foundation award, honorable
        mention: *The Year's Best Fantasy & Horror,* and *The
        Year's Best Science Fiction*
The Boy Who Bled Rubies
—first published *Don Juan and Men: Tales of Lust and Seduction,*
        MLR Press, 2009
A Kind Hand
— first published *Shroud Magazine #9,* 2009
The Fathomless World
—first published *Nemonymous 8: Cone Zero,* Nemonymous
        Press, 2008
The Fishwife
— first published *Descant #109,* 2000
Shoes
—previously unpublished, shortlisted for the Rannu fiction
        award, 2008

About the author:

Colleen Anderson has been nominated for two Aurora Awards, Gaylactic Spectrum Award, finalist in the Rannu competition and received several honorable mentions in the *Year's Best Fantasy and Horror*, the *Year's Best SF*, the *Year's Best Horror* and *Imaginarium*. Her poetry and fiction have been published in Britain, Canada and the United States. She has attended both the Clarion West and the Centre for the Study of Science Fiction (CSSF) writing workshops and has a degree in creative writing. Colleen is a member of the Horror Writers of America and SF Canada.

Connect with Colleen:

Blog: http://www.colleenanderson.wordpress.com
Facebook: http://www.facebook.com/colleen.anderson.9699
Smashwords:
https://www.smashwords.com/profile/view/ColleenAnderson
SF Canada:
http://www.sfcanada.org/index.php/sf-authors/62-colleen-anderson